the Journey of Rock ...

Four Guys, One Dream, One Stage

the Journey of Rock ...

Four Guys, One Dream, One Stage

Avishekh Das

Srishti
PUBLISHERS & DISTRIBUTORS

Srishti Publishers & Distributors
N-16, C. R. Park
New Delhi 110 019
srishtipublishers@gmail.com

First published by Srishti Publishers & Distributors in 2010

2nd impression, 2011

Typeset in AGaramond 11pt. by Suresh Kumar Sharma at Srishti

Printed and bound in India

Dedicated to my mom and dad

Acknowledgements

Phew! Finally this book sees the light of the day and I wish to thank many people who are associated with this book in some way or the other.

To begin with, thanks to my mom, dad and my brother for being my pillars of strength. This book would never have been a possibility without them.

For many a people, the book doesn't matter as much as the acknowledgement. Lest I be stoned or guillotined by these people, I want to thank them for the inspirational stories that they have inspired. My roommate Srikant, for being a blabbermouth. The night long discussions and criticisms helped me shape up this book. Thank you so much. A bunch of maniacs- Pratim Sengupta, Ankit Jain, Dhritik Nath, Sanyog Sharma, Kshitiz Kaushik and Abhishek Sharma for inspiring real life, adrenaline driven stories. Kudos to everyone. Thanks for being a part of my life.

Special thanks to Viky, Queen, Sonam and Kamal from whom I've learnt so many things in someway or the other.

All my cousins who have been so caring and supportive and for being there at every step. I owe my deepest gratitude to Sujoy Roy, Mrs. Deepa Sadula and Sourav Y for helping me with the cover.

All my fellow bloggers who take time to visit my virtual trash can. People of Guwahati, Shillong, Agra and the entire North-East, you guys are wonderful. Love you all. Not to forget my desktop and the sacrifices that it made in course of this beautiful journey.

Last but not the least, my publisher. The wonderful insights you provided me during our discussions which brought the best out of me. It would have been impossible without your valuable guidance. A grand thank-you to the entire team.

Finally, I thank the Almighty for having been so merciful and for showering his blessings upon me.

Of Khakis and love

"Shit! Forty-three kilos..?"

The spanking new weighing machine showed what I had just remarked. This was the worst thing that could have happened after the numerous failures in the entrance exams and love tales.

"Do you have anything to say on this?" I asked Prat, who was standing beside me watching the token pop out of the machine.

"Well, I would like to say that you are nothing but a piece of boneless chicken." Prat stated.

"Ha, ha......Mr. Satirist, see I'm laughing at your joke. Anyways thanks for reminding me."

I was a forty-three kilo moron trying my luck everywhere but every time, things just went the other way round. Welcome to the world of Samarth Dasgupta- an aspiring everything. I had, for the first time come to Guwahati, my home town after joining engineering two thousand kilometers away in Agra. I was a self-proclaimed vocalist of a fictitious band. It was three years ago that I first discovered my talent for singing English songs with élan and that was the only thing I wanted to do. What started as a rumor became my dream. But a noun, 'FATE' had other plans for me and here I was, trying to complete my engineering, struggling to cope up with the innumerable assignments, regular attendance, dumb professors and a low BMI.

Prat was my childhood friend and the only one who knew the secret that I was no vocalist; just a pretender and he kept mum. He was a budding engineer and gave me tips on how to tackle the internals and the externals.

"Got your tickets, dude?" he asked.

"Yeah, I checked that before leaving home." I assured Prat.

My vacations had ended and I was leaving for Agra. Prat had come with me to see me off. The last ten days would forever be etched in my memory.

"What do we do now?" he said.

"Let's check out if the train is on time." I suggested.

"Oh, Man! The Guwahati railway station has improved by leaps and bounds. I failed to notice that when I last came here. Look at those LCD screens and CCTV cameras." I said, standing in front of one of the cameras and throwing a kiss at it.

"Yeah, security has been tightened further after the recent bomb blasts." Prat explained.

"Ah! Fuck this violence, now I'm really tired of this." I commented.

"We can do nothing about this, we can only hope for a better future" he said.

"Hey, look at that pretty girl over there," I said, pointing towards a petite young girl sitting on a bench, sipping a cup of coffee.

She shared similarities with Rajeeta, my first crush and who I thought never left my mind though she left my life. It was two years since I last saw her.

"Yeah, she has resemblance with Rajeeta, doesn't she?" Prat asked sarcastically.

The worst thing was that Rajeeta's face appeared whenever I glanced at ninety-nine percent of the girls in the entire world.

"What do I do if her face appears at every point?" I said.

"You are a dumb-head" he said.

There was still one hour to go before departure and we decided on a cup of coffee.

"What do you plan to do?" Prat asked

"I do not have any idea right now but I'm searching for a drummer and a guitarist so that I can start a new band. But I'm really not sure whether I'll ever succeed in finding any." I said, feeling terrible that none of the bands would absorb me.

Music was my passion and I had learnt the art of singing on my own. I emulated singers like Cobain, Hetfield and Mustaine and if not perfectly, I came close. My greatest inspiration was Cobain and I developed a taste for grunge, the genre which Cobain developed and made it famous worldwide. Though there are innumerable Cobain critics, all lambasting him for his association with sex, drugs and alcohol, I, on the contrary, looked at the positive side. I was inspired by his music, not by the man himself. Like all great artists, I appreciated him for bringing in a revolution in the nineties rock scenario.

"Do not worry, Samarth, it's just a matters of time before you get an opportunity." He said, sympathizing for the great Samarth.

"But opportunity succeeds luck, isn't it?" I shot back.

"But you are lucky.....

"Who told you that? Guess you have little knowledge about people born on the thirteenth." I interrupted him mid way.

"That's shit man, British superstitions! Those maniacs were driven out fifty years ago" he said.

"Hope so!" I said. It was only hope that kept me alive.

"See Samarth, you are very talented, you have a good voice and you have got brains too. That in itself is a deadly combination" he said.

"Yeah, guess so!" I said.

"Come on, cheer up.....who knows, you might get hooked on to someone on the journey…" he said, trying to cheer me up.

"But, you know something, Prat?"

"Yeah, I know that you are a dumb-head" he smirked.

"Oh! Shut up, I'm really confused whether I have done the right thing or taken the right decision by opting engineering as a career option." I said.

"You have taken the right decision man...after all money is the fore most thing in a person's life...and in India, a person has to struggle from the very beginning and more so in the rock scene" he said.

"Yeah, I do agree with you."

"Hey, do you know that Dhritik proposed Tanisha yesterday?" Prat grinned.

"Oh, is that so? And did she accept his proposal?"

"She didn't say anything, she just signaled him." Prat said with the same grin on his face.

"What do you mean?"

"She showed him the same old middle finger." Prat said...laughing out loudly.

"What about Anushka? Are you still hanging on to her?" I asked Prat.

"Yup, I'm still with her."

"Are you really committed?"

"Actually I'm confused; I don't understand love and its complications. I do love her but sometimes she just eats the hell out of me....sometimes she bores me so much that I feel like jumping from the non-existent twin towers. I wish they existed" he said with a shrug.

"Does that mean that you are planning for something worse?" I asked Prat.

"Naa, nothing like that...she doesn't like my jokes...the other day I sarcastically asked her to pump in some money into my account as I couldn't afford phone bills any more...she did it...and the next day when I called her up...she asked me to pay my phone bills first...Miserable, isn't it?

"Tragic would be a better word."

"What about you? Did your search for Rajeeta? Prat asked, with a smirk on his face.

As Rajeeta was my first crush, I felt those tremendous adrenaline rushes whenever I looked at her. I was a teenager then and like any other, crushes were supposed to be love. I felt not only butterflies but hundreds of other creepy creatures tickling my gut and I felt ashamed of making my feelings clear to her. I was an introvert. I truly was.

It all started on the thirteenth of September when she brushed by my side and the perfume emitted was intoxicating. I turned around; saw her posterior, long dark hair moving slowly out of my sight. The next day, the first thing my eyes did, was to locate those similar locks of hair. I took the last bench...from where I could get almost the 180 degree view of the classroom. We were the newest batch and I hadn't made any friends yet. As my eyes scanned the entire classroom, they landed on the second bench. There she was, sitting right there, chatting away. I still hadn't seen her anterior but the love pangs had already started to show its colour. I was desperate to move out of the last seat and somehow get a seat in the first so that I could have a glimpse of the unknown. The teacher soon arrived and I decided to pretend a myopic.

"Sir, I'm a myopic, can I have a seat in the first row?"

Fortunately, the response was positive and the trick worked. I got a seat at the expense of another and I heaved a sigh of relief. The angle of rotation for my head was obtuse but it didn't matter. I turned my head and there she was, sitting right there, beautiful and my body metabolic rates increased like directly proportional graphs.

This continued for two months and whenever she gazed at me with her tiny blue eyes, I wished I were Superman. Finally after two long months I decided that the era of looking, peeping and gazing finally be over and a start to a new beginning be made. The classes ended and a positive frame of mind was built. She came out of the campus with her usual group of friends while I waited at the gate. As they passed the giant SONY showroom, I followed them, till her friends left and she was left all alone. I still didn't dare. I prayed louder and suddenly as if I attained Nirvana, I moved swiftly and uttered my quota of words.

"Hi! I am Samarth; may I know your name?"

She smiled, her face glowing. I knew her name but I needed to start somewhere.

"Hi! I'm Rajeeta." She stopped.

I was perspiring but that didn't stop me from moving my hands forward.

"Would you like to be my friend?" I asked her.

"Of course but we will talk tomorrow as I'm getting late."

If there wouldn't have been a single soul in the streets, I would have jumped a thousand feet into the air on hearing her answer. I was elated and as she left, I began planning for the future ahead. The next day we spent discussing our interests, likes and dislikes....all teenage gossip. The days passed and life rolled on but never could I gather enough courage to bare my heart in front of her.

I brought chocolates for her, which my young brother gobbled up while I was asleep before I could gift them and for days I couldn't afford another one due to the lack of funds. One winter day, I brought a packet of chocolate and I had to hide it on top of the ceiling fan.

Fortunately enough, my brother couldn't lay his hands on them though my entire room was raided in search of treasure. Next day, I packed it safely inside my bag but I was shocked to my core when she didn't come that day. I was dejected but I hoped to gift it the next day. She was absent again and I had to take it back. She was absent for the next four days. On the sixth day, while I was asleep, my brother raided my room again, switched on the fan, the chocolate box fell down and with one stroke, he grabbed it and disappeared. I could do nothing but just stare as he gobbled up the entire packet. The next day, she had come and rest is history.

The college days were about to end but still I hadn't said a word to her. I decided to bare my heart out once I got admission in one of the prestigious colleges, but the day never saw the light. I got admitted at a college at Agra after cracking an all India entrance. I called her but the landline had been disconnected. I waited and waited and waited for two more years, which I spent searching for her but never could I find her anywhere. Then I found Shreya, She was a gift which I thought I would treasure for the rest of my life.

"Hey! day dreaming again?" Prat said.

"Oh! I'm sorry, my mind just drifted into the past and please don't remind me of her...her name gives me jitters now. Do you know what happened the day before yesterday?"

"What?"

"As usual, I woke up early in the morning and set out on a mission- a mission to find out my love. The irony in this story is that there's a police station right opposite to her college. As I was waiting for her to come out, I saw three people, all of them khaki clad, approaching me. I stood there waiting for them to pounce upon me. They began asking me the reasons about what I was doing here."

"I told you not to wear that damn Burmese cargo of yours. You look like a terrorist in that attire. What happened then? What did you tell them?"

"I told them, I was waiting for my sister to come out."

"And did she come out?"

"That's the worst part, I awaited her till four in the evening but she never came out."

"I'm eager to listen to the worst part Samarth."

"The policemen returned, I shuddered and seeing them, I flew past the multitudes, faster than the speed of light." I continued my story.

"Wow! People really develop wings when police are behind them, don't they?" Prat asked, trying to make a joke out of it.

"Good joke, mate"

"Will you let me continue my story?"

"Yup, sure, carry on..."

"As I made a mad dash, I imagined myself inside an Indian prison full of hardened criminals and the very thought of spending my time with them sent shivers down my spine. I ran even faster, the police still behind me. Half a kilometer into the chase, I saw a familiar face of a girl ahead of me. She was walking straight towards me."

"Shit! I think I know who that was..."

"And you have guessed correctly. That was the very girl; I was waiting for all day, Rajeeta, the love of my life."

She looked beautiful. A strand of hair fell down right across her face. As I rushed past her, it felt as if a thousand pound bunker busting bomb was pounding in my heart. It pained so much so that I could feel it scream as if an African elephant had stepped on it. But I couldn't stop. My life was more important to me than those three golden words which I planned to tell her.

"Didn't she notice you?"

"May be she did, may be she didn't' I replied.

"What do you mean by that?" Prat asked me again.

"The fact is that, I didn't turn around to look at her." I said.

"What happened after that?" Prat asked excitedly

I ran even faster, my heart pumping. There was a square ahead of me. I decided to turn left, than right, no left would be a better option. Poor decision making skills can be destructive. Finally, I turned left. Right ahead of me, I saw another familiar face, sitting on a scooter, puffing away. It was Lucky. He was my classmate. I called out to him. He saw me, his face turned blue.

"Start your jet." I screamed.

Kick 1, kick 2, kick 3- it wouldn't start and I thought we were dead. The police were right behind us....charging at us like bulls charge at matadors and *lathis* ready to beat the hell out of us. Finally the jet started, I became a pillion rider and then bang-darkness prevailed.

I woke up only to find myself in a hospital room, Lucky in the adjacent bed. Mom was sitting right next to me and dad- his face red, looking at me in disgrace. Later I was discharged with a swollen thigh and an inch long cut on top of my left eyebrow.

"That was horrible, but....

"I know you are going to ask me what happened in the middle....." I interrupted Prat.

"Yeah...." Prat said.

One of the policemen had come so close that one swing of his *lathi* hit me in the right arm. I panicked and in this hullabaloo, Lucky lost control of his scooter. The scooter rammed against a car parked near a wide uncovered drain. Like a tennis ball, I bounced high up in the air and landed straight in the drain. The drain water acted as a cushion and this saved me from leaving for the heavens above. Lucky had a fractured thumb and a wound on his left shoulder. After this incident, he promised he would never talk to me ever again. I fell unconscious and police brought us to this hospital, informed our parents and there we were lying disgraced. More fuel was added to fire, when the police fined us a thousand bucks and dad had to pay the entire amount.

"Gosh, what a story..." Prat stated.

P-o-o-o-o..........the train was ready to leave.

"Oh! I think the train is ready to leave, now let me take my seat lest someone else try to lay his hands on it" I said.

'See you then, bye, wish you a pleasant journey" Prat said.

"Bye, enjoy your life" I wished him back.

I wished Prat goodbye and set out for a long journey. I never knew that this train journey would forever change my life.

Journey of Eternity

The train was almost empty. Hooking up, seemed to be a forgone conclusion. Girls were almost becoming a rarity on trains now. As always I took the window seat. The train started rolling out of the station.

Besides me, there were three other passengers in my compartment. A young Manipuri guy sat on the opposite seat. Another man, whose face starkly reminded me of Tom Hanks from the movie 'Saving Private Ryan', sat beside him. The third one, sitting beside me was a soldier although it was mere guesswork going by his looks. He kept a Verrappan like moustache and for once I thought he had risen from his tomb and shifted to Assam.

The journey was a long one, 32 hours to be precise but then, we were at the mercy of the train driver. For the next 31.5 hours, he would be our God.

As the train passed by the busy streets of Guwahati, I felt nostalgic. Pleasant memories of my stay at this lovely city came flowing by. I would really miss those lip-smacking momos, the serene Brahmaputra, the misty hills, the khaki clad *mushtandas* and above all, my girl.

The sky was crystal clear and the silvery water of the only male river glistened in the morning sun. The arrival of the TTE awakened from my journey down memory lane.

"Ticket please" he said. I handed over my ticket to him. He had a good look at it before proceeding to check the Manipuri guy's ticket.

The guy handed over to him a parchment which I recognized was a local train ticket.

"This isn't the right one. Show me the right one" he said.

TTE's generally are a ruthless lot. They pounce at any opportunity where they can lay their hands on a ticket less person. I sensed that the guy had landed in trouble. Apparently, he was travelling in a train for the first time. I had faced a similar situation before and I knew that bribe along with a hefty fine was the only way out. The guy was helpless. That's when I decided to step in.

"You pay him the fine and add a couple of hundred more and he'll let you off" I said, whispering into his ears.

The guy shelled out a sum of seven hundred and fifty and the TTE let him off. It was quite a bargain.

"Hi, I'm Jerry" he introduced himself.

Talking to strangers on trains was a strict no-no but this guy was different.

"Hi, I'm Samarth" I said as I shook hands with him.

"You are an army man, aren't you?" he asked.

I was surprised. *An army man..?* I never expected this remark. *Didn't he notice my low BMI?* I really had no idea what made him think like that but inside I felt happy that there were at least some people in this world who didn't care about my skinny figure after all.

"No, I'm doing my B.Tech from Agra" I said. India is a production house of engineers and I was just one of those moronic products.

"Whoa! I wanted to be an engineer too but I couldn't get through one of those entrance exams" he said.

"What do you do then?" I asked.

"I work at a call center in Gurgaon" he said.

Call center..? These two words freaked me out. I didn't know the exact reason but the incidences and the co-incidences reported in the newspapers were enough to hold me back from experiencing them. The reason might also have been because sometimes you tend to develop false notions about things you have never experienced.

"Actually this is the first time that I'm travelling in a train. Shall we pass through Bihar?" Jerry said.

I, at once, understood his question. Every first-timer is terrified at the prospect of spending a night in Bihar.

"Yes, it will but you need not fear about anything. Bihar is largely peaceful" I said.

What I didn't tell him was the fact that although Bihar was peaceful, trains weren't. I mean, when eunuchs rule the roost, can anyone rule a kingdom? The answer is a big NO.

We had already covered up three hours of the total journey. The sun was almost overhead and the temperature was soaring. I decided to take a nap.

My cock-a-doodle clock sounded. It was an antique piece of time ware gifted to me by my granny when I had appeared for my boards. It sometimes did mess up with the mornings and the dusks but none the less, it did manage to wake me up almost every exam day. It was my most trusted associate.

I woke up. My eyes were still shut when I noticed Jerry holding a guitar like object. On further scrutiny, I found that it was indeed a guitar.

"So, you like playing the guitar" I said.

"Yep, the guitar is my best friend" he answered.

The sound of the six-string always mesmerized me. As I watched him, my thoughts went back to my school days when I held the status of being a vocalist. As the days passed by, this lie risked being blown apart. So, I was left with only one option- either be a vocalist or die of shame.

Jerry started strumming on his guitar. He was playing a song which I recognized was 'Lying Eyes' by the Eagles. The Tom Hanks look-alike watched him in awe while the soldier seemed disinterested.

"I love this song" I said. He said nothing but continued playing the song.

"I have a dream. I always wanted to have my own band" I said.

He gave me a dazzled look probably because a few moments ago I was as silent as a lamb and suddenly I was hurling at him a volley of statements. I sensed that he was a guitarist. He was flawless with the chords. Prat had told me that there was a probability of getting hooked and it was coming true. I was getting hooked to Jerry and his guitar skills.

"Do you like Nirvana?" he asked.

Bingo. He was a fan of the legendary Kurt Cobain. I too was.

"I am a huge fan of Nirvana. In fact, it's my favourite band" I said.

"Do you know the song 'Penny royal tea" he said.

Before I could say yes, he had already started playing the song. I thought Jerry was an avatar of Cobain himself.

As Jerry continued playing, I looked through the window. The sky was getting dark with every passing second. As Jerry ended the song, the train came to a screeching halt. There were paddy fields on both sides which extended to infinity. At least it seemed so. At the distant, I could see lights. A city was near.

The train started moving albeit at a snails pace and finally it entered into a large station.

"Which station is it?" Jerry asked.

Jerry had some bad news in store for him. We were in Bihar.

"Katihar" I said with a shrug.

More bad news was pouring in. The train was abuzz with rumours that a goods train had collided with another one and both had turned turtle. Rumours tend to be true in these parts and Jerry got the shock of his life when he came to know that we had to spend the night in the station.

I decided to take a stroll. I invited Jerry but he was too terrified to step out of the train. I decided to venture out alone. The station was teeming with passengers, chaiwallahs and every kind of eatable-wallahs.

I was checking out some books at a bookstore when someone tugged my shirt from behind. I turned around only to find Jerry standing with his guitar.

"It feels sick to be alone" he said.

"Yes, it does Mr. Lonely" I said.

Together, we checked out a couple of books along with a couple of ladies.

"Coffee..?" I asked. Jerry nodded.

"I want to be a vocalist" I said as I ordered two cups of coffee. Jerry wasn't surprised. Fifty percent of rock music enthusiasts want to be a vocalist.

"Is it? I want to form a band too. There are few listeners in Gurgaon and I'm passionate about music" he said.

"Gurgaon and Agra isn't far away from each other. Why don't we form a band of our own?" I said, as I sipped my cup of coffee, almost burning my tongue in the process.

"Good idea, but I'll have to think about it" he said.

We were sitting on one of the railings of a railway over bridge when Jerry once again began strumming on his guitar.

"Would you like to jam-in with me?" he said.

I was elated though I refused to sing an English song. I feared it might just raise quite a few eyebrows.

"Can you sing Dooba by Silk Route?" he said.

"Yea, I can" I said.

As he started playing the initial chords, a small crowd gathered in our vicinity. As I started singing, the station was filled with the sounds of the beautiful song. The crowd was growing larger with time and as I ended the song the sound of laughter echoed through the station. People thought that we were a bunch of clowns who had disappeared from some circus. That was their definition of musician on the rocks. It was certain that they had never seen anyone performing a duet.

I and Jerry quietly moved out of their sight. The clock struck eleven and there was still no certainty when the journey would resume. We both decided to sleep for sometime.

She looked beautiful. She was wearing a green salwar-kameez and when she entered my dark room, it almost lit up. In a few minutes she would be in my arms. I would embrace her and never let her slip away. I could see her mystifying eyes. My heart beat faster as she came close to me. I could almost touch her and feel her warm body.

I woke up with a jerk. I felt someone tugging at my shirt. All this while, I was dreaming about Rajeeta. I turned around. I froze as I saw him.

"*Paisa de de baba*" his shrill voice almost got onto my nerves. A *eunuch in the middle of the night..*? I had never expected this. I tried to find Jerry. He was nowhere to be seen. I pulled out a ten rupee note and handed it to him.

"I want fifty rupees" he said. This was extortion. I refused his demand but he was adamant. As I began to climb down from my upper berth, he began accosting me. More than being accosted, I feared being molested. Before he would slip his hands inside my shirt, I pulled out a fifty rupee note and handed it over to him. He quietly turned around and went his way.

I climbed down from my berth to find Jerry. He crawled out from under his seat.

"What was that?" he said. He was probably shaken by the appearance of the extortionist.

"That was something you would never like to stumble upon any time in your life" I said. I realized that Jerry was disgruntled. After a few funny anecdotes, we decided to retire for the night.

Rem

The stage is set. The crowd is roaring. I step into the stage. As I watch the crowd, I try to estimate their number, maybe around half a million. My dream has at last come true. Jerry strums his guitar. The intro is great. The response is amazing. A Mexican wave runs through the crowd, shivers, down my spine. I find no meaning in the song but the crowd loves it. Suddenly the legendary figure of Kurt Cobain appears from nowhere. I feel like I'm dreaming. He is long dead. But maybe I'm dreaming. No, I'm not in the virtual world. We sing together in unison...

Give me Leonard Cohen afterworld......
Sit and drink pennyroyal tea......

Suddenly, the sky is raining fire. Giant fireballs descend from the sky and hit the earth. People start screaming and running helter-skelter. I watch in trepidation as the figure of Kurt Cobain vanishes into thin air. I try to stop him but in vain. Jerry is still playing the guitar. He is in a trance. *Is he not noticing these giant fireballs*? The stage catches fire. I try to run but soon I get engulfed in thick flames. The lights go out. Everything goes dark.

Suddenly I felt Jerry jerking me violently. I woke up only to find myself perspiring.

"Dreaming, huh?"

"Yeah, sweet and bitter, you can say..."

I checked out my watch. It was three in the morning. I decided to sleep a little more.

As the first lights appeared, I woke up only to find Jerry having his breakfast.

"Good morning, Samarth..."

"Good morning, Jerry..."

"You had a horrible dream, isn't it?

"Not exactly, it had a sweet beginning but the end was not very great."

"Coffee..?" Jerry asked

"Naa, I would like to have a cup of tea."

As we both, sipped a cup of hot tea, we discussed our plans to start a new band.

"But we would need a good drummer and a bassist." I suggested.

"Yea, we sure have to find them"

We knew, we both were small town guys and running after our dreams won't be easy.

"Jerry, why do you like rock so much? I said.

"I don't know, may be because of the environment in which I grew up. There was violence all around and people were famished. So, when I started listening rock, it made me feel at peace. It calmed my nerves. It acted as a drug" Jerry said.

"It was the same with me; the first five years of my childhood was full of happiness and than the trouble started" I said.

"But how did you take up the guitar?" I asked.

"I learnt it from the age of eight thanks to my boss that I now have mastered it" he answered. It was then Jerry unraveled the mystery of his boss and his relation with the guitar.

Tom's and Jerry Reloaded

My cock-a-doodle beeped. I checked out my watch. It showed 7.30. The train hadn't moved an inch. I poked Jerry on his waist. He woke up with a jerk and rubbed his eyes like a six year old kid.

"Where are we?" he asked.

"In the midst of heaven and hell, I mean, we are still at Katihar" I said with a chuckle.

"Seems like it's going to be one long journey" Jerry said.

"A journey of eternity" I said.

"I had a strange dream…." I continued.

"Dreams reflect your passion" Jerry remarked after I narrated him my dream.

"How did you take up the guitar?" I asked Jerry.

"It's a long story" Jerry said.

A long story…? I loved listening to tales and nothing amused me more than teenage love stories and of course, sex. Sex, because I was a loser, a virgin, and still a no-hoper all according to my dearest Prat.

"I would love to hear your story" I said.

Aventrix, one of the largest call centers in Gurgaon, was home to 1300 employees and Jerry was one among them. Neslie was Jerry's supervisor. To be a little more honest, I need to confess that Neslie was Jerry's boss and even worse- a nymphomaniac. It's a derogatory term but what would you call a woman who tries to seduce seventy one men in one single week?

"Oh! Come on, Jerry, I need a favour" Neslie said.

"Favour?" *I'm dead.*

Jerry raised his eyebrows and his face turned pale with fear. Rumors abounded that Neslie had tried to rape seven of her male employees in the last seven days. Jerry was on course to be the eighth. The worse was yet to come.

"Have a seat Mr. Handsome" she said in a soft but bitchy tone.

Jerry sat down. He knew he was in something real bad, something worse than he could imagine.

"Here, take these files" Neslie said, as she handed to him a stack of files.

"I'm fond of being fondled" she continued further. Jerry stared at her and his eyes fell on her size 38 tits.

"I know what you are looking at naughty boy" she said. *I'm looking at an ugly pair of headlights with no lights in them.*

"Now come on, feel free and do whatever you want to" Neslie said as she came closer to Jerry.

"Ma'am, I've loads of work waiting for me" Jerry said.

"No work is more important than me" Neslie said as she got up and moved her lips within inches of Jerry's already pale face. Getting raped was the last thing he ever wanted but on the other hand, he didn't want to loose his plum job.

Neslie held his hand and skid it inside her shirt. *Feels like a cherry on top of a huge jackfruit.*

As I sat listening to Jerry and his unusual sexual escapade, I heard a faint sound of a clap.

"Shhh...!" I signaled Jerry.

I peeped out through the window only to see some unknown but familiar faces.

"Oh! O', they are coming" I said.

"Who is coming? Jerry said. He seemed confused.

"A bunch of dumb headed transsexuals" I said.

No sooner, Jerry heard this; he hurriedly crawled under his seat.

"They will find you here; I have a plan" I whispered.

I had a plan for every situation but they seldom worked. A mouthful of expletives beautifully graced was what I always received after numerous such plans failed to work. Nonetheless, I decided to give it a shot.

"Here's the plan. We both run towards the opposite directions and enter two different toilets. Bolt the door from inside. As soon as these pieces of shit take their asses out of here, we go back and you continue your story" I said, almost sounding like a war-veteran.

As the sound of clapping got a bit louder, I signaled Jerry to run. He dashed off like a mad bull.

"Keep your phone on" I shouted as I negotiated my way though piles of luggage stocked on my way. I turned around only to find Jerry disappear inside one of the toilets. I entered into inside one of the less stinky ones, bolted the door from inside and waited.

As Jerry entered inside, he froze. A pair of hands grabbed him by his shoulders and pinned him against the wall. His shoulders ached as he tied to regain his composure. Jerry was trapped inside a train toilet with a trans-sexual and she/he seemed horny. *You can run, you can hide but you can't escape my love,* the lyrics of Enrique Iglesius's famous song Escape echoed inside Jerry's brain. The trans-sexual brushed his/her hand against the most sensitive part of Jerry's anatomy. Jerry tried to free himself of his/her grip but the eunuchs' strong muscular arms made sure that the prey could not escape his/her clutches.

I was still waiting for the ordeal to end when my cell beeped. It was Jerry and I picked up the call.

"Enjoying the stink..?" I said. I waited for Jerry's reply but there was none. There was no answer or the question was pretty tough to answer.

"Is everything all right?" I said again. I heard some whooshing sounds and I could guess that Jerry was entangled in a lip-lock. *Sex inside a train toilet - unbelievable.*

"Carry on brother, I knew you would get hooked" I said. I cut the line feeling happy that Cupid had found the bull's eye.

As soon as I hung up, my cell beeped again. Jerry's number flashed on the screen. I wondered what it was. Expecting a hello, I picked up the call.

"Ah...! Hell...ppp..." Jerry screamed. Jerry had landed in trouble. Without much deliberation, I rushed out for a rescue mission.

"My name is Champa" he/she introduced himself/herself. Jerry tried to free himself.

"I'll call the police if you do not let me go" Jerry warned him/her.

The trans-sexual was still holding on to his body in a tight grip.

"A thousand rupees and I would let you go" Champa said as he/she started unzipping Jerry's trousers. Jerry smelt freedom. *This is my chance.*

"I can pay you only if you let me bring the money" he said. Champa's eyes glimmered. *A thousand bucks..?*

"Remember one thing- act smart and I'll slit your throat" Champa said as he/she let Jerry off.

"You only have a minute" Champa said as Jerry rushed out of the toilet.

I was completely out of breath as I reached the toilet where Jerry was hiding. There was no sign of him. I knocked on the door. The door opened slowly and the sight inside made my heart skip a beat. A transsexual stood right there smiling at me. My pounding heart almost stopped beating and I had no other way than to find another way. Jerry was nowhere to be seen either.

I stepped out of the train and into the station. Often, people are abducted for ransom in these parts. *What if they had turned Jerry into one of their own kinds*? These thoughts sent shivers down my spine.

The train finally readied to leave. I wondered where Jerry was. Deep inside, fear struck me and the fear turned into a worst case scenario when, I saw Jerry on the run. He was being chased by three muscular, six feet tall eunuchs, all ready to slit his throat. The state of affairs turned for the worse when the train began pulling out off the station slowly but surely. *I need to do something.*

My hands trembling, I picked up my phone and dialed Jerry's number. The train was catching up speed and I jumped into it.

"It's not the right time to have a discussion" Jerry said, as soon as he picked up my call.

"Get on the train, lest you want to be a dead rat" I said.

"I need to get these guys off my back, but how?" Jerry screamed on the phone with such intensity that it would almost have busted my dear ear drums had I not unplugged my headphones at the right time.

"Listen to me carefully…"

"No more plans please….I have been traumatized enough" Jerry interrupted me midway.

"Distract them. Throw your phone and climb into the train…it's still running at 30kms/hr" I said, trying to force the idea into his mind.

"Do you even know how much an N-93 costs?" he yelled at me.

"Then I better prepare for your funeral" I said and hung up. Then I prayed as I gawked through the door for any signs of Jerry. My guts told me that he had done it and they were right.

Ten minutes later he was standing right beside me as he gasped for each breath. The train had caught enough speed now and the eunuchs were left behind. We thanked the Lord as we made our way through the long passage into our berths.

"I need a glass of water". Jerry was still panting.

"Seems like we are in trouble" I shrugged as I desperately searched for my crimson red Reebok bag. My bag had disappeared. So had Jerry's.

Fortunately, my wealth lay safe in my bank, all thanks to the ATM and unfortunately, Jerry lost his brand new I-pod, his 320 GB external hard drive and a collection of Armani lingerie in addition to his N-93. Looking at his face, I could now define 'traumatized' near perfectly. *Good old Champa*. She had the last laugh.

The entire fault lay within me. My plan failed to work yet again and I had no excuses. I hated paying for things I never stole and more so for things I stole. After all, stealing is a job for which you do not pay. I had to find an excuse. The Tom Hanks look alike had shifted into another compartment while the Verrappan look alike lay on the upper berth sleeping like a dead snake. I decided to be a vulture. Before Jerry would pop a question, I blurted.

"He could have saved the day for us" I said, pointing to the Verrappan look alike. Jerry looked at me in disgust. It is not very easy to shift the entire blame on someone who has nothing to do with it in the first place. But I tried and I had to. After a ten minute long explanation, I finally succeeded in convincing Jerry that the Verrappan look alike was entirely responsible for all the mess that we were in. Strangely, Jerry believed me. Maybe, I was too hot to handle.

Nevertheless, the good news was that, Jerry decided to forget about the things that he lost and counted the positives. He had gained a friend. Me. We decided to start our own band and play our original compositions. Rock once again dominated our discussion. Neslie came back.

"Sit back, relax and listen to my tragic tale" Jerry said, as he wiped away the sweat that had amassed just above his eyebrows.

"What happened with the cherry and the jackfruit?" I said.

Neslie was on a high and she meant business. Jerry hands were now entwined firmly inside her shirt. Her hands slowly made their way inside Jerry's shirt and reached his bums. Jerry closed his eyes and prayed. Fortunately, God answered. A loud knock on the door cut short the erotic session.

"Stay right there" Neslie said, as she leapt back onto her chair.

"Come in"

"The boss wants to see you" a messenger told her.

"I'm coming in just a minute" Neslie replied. Jerry heaved a sigh of relief.

"You are so unfortunate but I have a better idea" Neslie said. Jerry understood that he was in for a bigger surprise.

"Every night you will play the guitar for me. You can start tonight" Neslie said. She was unforgiving.

"But Ma'am, I'm not skillful enough" Jerry mumbled as Neslie skirted out of the door.

"Then learn it" she said, with a look of disdain. It was an order.

Although, Jerry had learnt playing the six-string, he wasn't adept at it. The next six months, he spent learning and improvising his skills along with entertaining Neslie not to mention his one night stands. He was addicted, addicted to the cherries and the jackfruits which he once detested. He was now a maestro. Neslie had turned out to be a blessing in disguise.

"Man! Are you still hanging around Neslie?" I said after he completed his story.

"Yeah, she's still my boss" he said.

So this was it, adventures all the way. I proposed to start our own band and Jerry instantly agreed. We decided to meet the following month and plan things out. We would need a drummer and a bassist and the way things were going, I was pretty sure that Fate was leading me to where I belonged. Agra finally beckoned and so did aplenty surprises.

Instinctive Fatass

Agra- a day later:
Homesickness had finally settled in.

It was seven in the morning when I heard a loud knock on the door. All night, I had been dreaming about Cobain performing alongside me until a giant fireball descended from the sky destroying the entire stage. I realized that this was a repetition of the dream which I had in the train. My eyes were still shut and I almost dragged myself towards the door and opened it.

"Hey, thin ass back from home?" Armi said as he pushed me aside and entered the room.

"Hi, Armi nice to see you again" I said generating a fake smile on my face.

"Seems you have finally found your love" he said as he went straight towards the bed and started juggling two brand new mugs which were so dearly packed into my bag by mom.

"No man, once again history repeated itself" I said.

"Then why are you smiling?" he asked, as he continued juggling the mugs.

Armi alias Armaan Sharma was my best friend, my classmate and my neighbor. We lived in the same hostel which was a stones throw away from the college building. The only thing common between the both of us was the fact that like me, he too didn't have an ounce of idea why he had joined engineering.

"You are a born juggler….

I still hadn't completed my sentence when one of the jugs came crashing down. Luckily, the other one fell straight into the bed. Armi smiled his thirty two whites fully visible.

"I'm sorry" he said, as he collected the bits and pieces of the broken chinaware scattered all over the floor.

"It's fine. I brought two because I knew this was going to happen" I said.

"Man, this semester will screw us, we have got our core subjects coming up- G.E (Genetic Engineering), Biotech, Biochemistry etc. etc."

I just forgot to mention people but we were doing our bachelors in Biotechnology, the worst branch of engineering one could possibly land upon.

Coming back to Armaan, he was a chain smoker with his daily cigarette consumption going up to three packets. I was a passive smoker and the amount of smoke I inhaled was much more than Armi inhaled in an entire day. This way I risked dying sooner than Armi. I tried to smoke Armi out every time he lighted up in my room but instead I got smoked out. Finally, after seven months of agony and hundreds of unsuccessful attempts to get rid of his smoking habit, I was left with only one option- switch to smoking myself. That way, at least I wouldn't have to repent the fact that I had never tasted a cigarette before death.

Anyways, the ultimate gelling point between the two of us was that he was a fat ass and I a thin ass, although that was his point of view.

When Armi first came to Agra, he never quite mixed with people, was studious enough, scoring high grades in almost all the subjects although cigarettes were his bread and butter and he couldn't live without the '*agarbattis*' as he usually called them. He liked north-easterners though which I could gauge from the fact that the first person whom he befriended was me. There was another reason- ragging.

We were made to dance together under the same roof. I was made the heroine wearing a night gown and Armi was made to wear a *dhoti.* Together we made a pretty good couple. In the Fresher's day, we bumped into the same girl who unfortunately turned out to be our senior. That night we ran for our lives and ended up spending the night in one of the rice fields in the outskirts of Agra. Those were our first year days and slowly and steadily, we became the closest of friends.

As the days passed, Armi changed to become more of a sadistic pleasure as I watched him shred everyone's ego into bits and massacre mosquitoes that dwelled in his room.

Obviously, people change when they live in the company of Samarth. When I asked Armi teasingly why he had changed in just a matter of months, he replied "you are the bloody reason". He accused me for of this change. He even changed the adage- 'an idle mind is a devils workshop' to 'an idle mind is Samarth's workshop' making the devil and Samarth sound synonymous. I didn't care. The reason was simple. Armi had a huge physique and every time I messed up with someone he was there to rescue me. I called this 'protectionism'.

The only time of the day when he hated me was between 4:30 and 9:00 in the evening. Reason- it was my daily dose of Cobain from 4.30 to 9.30 with decibel intensity going up to the level of eardrums being battered and shattered. A Himesh Reshamiya fan to the highest pitch possible, he disliked 'my kinda music' which generally consisted of grunge, thrash metal and alternative rock.

But still we were the best of friends and he would do anything and everything for me. I coined his name Armi partly because it sounded like the shorter version of Armaan and partly because his dad was a retired lieutenant colonel in the Indian Army.

"Samarth, will your daydreams ever cease" he said, shaking me vigorously.

"Actually Armi, I was thinking about the past two years which we have spent together" I said, as I saw him browsing through the porn stuff hidden in my computer.

"Don't think about that. You have already made my life hell and I do not want to ruin it further. By the way, my instincts tell me that something is going on in your mind. May be you are up to some pranks or something" he said, sneering at me.

"No, mate, there is nothing like there is nothing like that" I said.

Mr. Fatass always blabbers about his supra normal talent- his natural ability to sniff out dangers which can even put German Sheppard's to shame. He has this uncanny ability to sniff out dangers, which saved my life not once, not twice but thrice. Thanks Mr. Fatass.

We were opposite to each other in every aspect but as Coulomb's law says equal and opposite attracts each other, this seemed true in case of me and Armi.

"Do you remember my first kiss?" I asked.

"Yuck! That was the worst that could have happened" Armi said.

"Did you bring what I asked you to?" he asked.

"Yes, I did" I said, as I pulled out a pair of brand new Levi sneakers from my bag.

"Oh, how beautiful it is" he said, as he put them on and began jumping up and down like a little kid.

He wanted to look ultra-glam and this was the first step towards that direction. He was enjoying his new avatar.

"Thank you so much, I have to go" he said and left me alone.

"Good bye" I wished him back.

A Kissful Night

As Armi left, I closed the door and sank into the chair. The past few months could have been devastating for me. But Mr. Fatass was always there every time I landed in trouble. It was in this very room that I had my first kiss, a daredevil attempt even Heath Ledger would not have dared to perform out of his reel life.

It was just another day the only difference being that our third semester exams were going on and everyone was busy studying as we had PCC (Process Calculations), the toughest paper one could come across the next day. Teachers had already predicted that seventy percent of the students would fail in this subject. This made us turn from being a one-night fighter to a three-night fighter.

Studies became the most important aspect of our lives. Our parents would really have been proud of us had they been around at this time of the year. Although most of the students carried with them a bundle of 'micro-minis' better known as 'pharrahs' which contained the entire book, for Armi and me it was an unholy act. Also we had discovered a noble way to substitute the 'pharrahs'. How? We made the best use of the palms of our hands and the tiny admit card. Longer equations were shortened and formulae compressed to fit in them.

It was almost eight in the evening. The sun had just set and there was still seventeen more hours to go before the nightmarish experience was to commence. I had been studying for about three hours and I decided to take a break. I put my ear on the wall. I could hear Armi studying, in fact, cramming up the notes. I had grown tired of all the chemistry shit that I was cramming up since the last two days but Armi seemed determined. After five backlogs in the first two semesters, he desperately wanted to gift himself a clean mark sheet this time.

"Hey, don't you try to spy on me Samarth", pat came the reply from the other side, no sooner had I put my ears on the wall.

Man, this bloody bastard has real strong instincts.

"Would you like to play a game of FIFA with me" I asked. Armi had recently installed FIFA in his computer.

"Shut up and go to work" pat came the reply once again.

My primary objective was to disturb him. . I followed a very simple funda - when Samarth does not study, no one should.

Armi was a movie freak. Even infra-sounds of the 'Lord of the rings' or 'A walk to remember' could make Armi's concentration go weak. I turned on the computer and played the movie. I waited for a reaction. Ten minutes passed and I was still waiting. There wasn't any response. Fifteen minutes later I turned off the computer.

I decided to switch over to plan-B. This plan had everything in it to prevent Armi from getting his job done. Once again, I turned on the computer. This time I played Cobain. Slowly, I increased the sound till the decibel level reached its critical point. I put my ear on the wall but I could hear nothing, not even a murmur. At last I had tasted success. I sat down on the chair. A loud knock on the door interrupted the momentous occasion.

I opened the door. I knew the devil had arrived but instead I found three guys standing. I at once identified them as my seniors. A shiver ran down my spine. Before I could say anything, one of the punched me straight on my face. I fell down with a thud. I lay down groaning in pain.

"Shut down the computer" one of them barked.

I scrambled towards the computer and turned it off.

"Never ever try to disturb us again" they said as they left the room.

Plan-B had terribly gone wrong. I sank into the chair again. I heard someone giggling. It was Armi. He stood outside my room enjoying every bit of the drama that had just unfolded. I felt insulted and this was killing me. I could do nothing but smirk at him. I wished Armi would be out of my sight. Finally after nine agonizing minutes, he went back to his room. Armi proved that he was a tough nut to crack.

I closed the door and sank into the chair once again. My dry throat irritated me. I picked up a bottle of water kept beside the computer and lo...I was choking. My epiglottis had jammed. I couldn't inhale air. I was breathless. Five seconds passed. I started coughing. I needed help. My lungs seemed to burst out. The pain in my chest was unbearable. Ten seconds passed but there was no sign of relief. The atmosphere seemed to be devoid of oxygen.

My muddled up brain thought of Armi. *Wasn't he listening? May be he was thinking of this as yet another prank.*

I was slowly but surely suffering an aneurysm. I wished life gave me another chance. Slowly and steadily, I was loosing all hope. I collapsed. A flashback of all the deeds I had done in my life played in my fuzzy brain.

Five seconds later, an angel appeared from nowhere. My face had turned pale and my pupils constricted to the point where I could see only shadows. I couldn't recognize that angel.

The angel picked me up. I thought I had died and the angel had come to throw me into the burning flame of hell. But what he did amazed me.

The angel caught hold of me and pushed his lips across mine. I felt air gushing into my oxygen starved lungs. I fell unconscious.

I woke up only to find Armi standing beside me puffing away. A smile stretched across his face and I realized that the angel was none other than Armi.

"Congratulations" he said.

"What for..?" I asked.

"You just had your first kiss" he said with a smirk on his face.

"Yuck! You are not my girlfriend" I said.

"Of course not, I'm your saviour" he said.

For the next half an hour, I threw a million curses at him but at the end, I hugged him. Tears came rolling down my eyes. I had the closest encounter with death.

The Gay Encounter

It was 1:30pm and I was sitting in the examination hall, beside the window in the ground floor. I hadn't slept the whole night. Sleep was now creeping into my eyes. Armi was sitting in the adjacent room. We had decided to meet at the toilet exactly one and a half hour after the commencement of the exam to clarify any doubts. I looked at the invigilator. He seemed strict.

I wasn't carrying any 'pharrahs' and so had nothing to fear about. Five minutes later, the invigilator distributed the question paper. The first thing that went through my mind on analyzing the question paper carefully was-'I'm screwed up'. Of the eight questions in all, I could answer only two. I wondered how Armi was doing. For the first time in three semesters, I missed 'pharrahs'. I began jotting down the answers.

Forty-five minutes later, I finished my first answer. I checked my watch. There was time, a total of two hours and eight minutes. The second question was tougher. I was stuck in the middle. The neurons of my brain stopped co-operating. There was nothing much I could do except to hope for a miracle.

One and a half hour passed and the time arrived to meet Armi. I got up, took the invigilator's permission and walked outside. There were not many people around. I waited for Armi. Five minutes passed but Armi didn't come. Dejected on being backstabbed, I returned to my room.

As I sat down, a hand popped in from outside the window. The hand was gripping tightly a bundle of pharrahs. I was shocked at the first instance but regained my composure on seeing Armi holding them. I quickly grabbed them and slid them inside my pocket. The invigilator hadn't noticed me and I let a sigh of relief. Now there was a chance that I could somehow scrape through the thirty mark barrier.

Sensing an opportunity, I quickly opened one of the pharrahs and started copying the answers. I quickly finished the second question and moved on to the third. The answer to the third one was longer than the first two and I started jotting it down, all the time keeping an eye on the invigilator.

I had almost finished the third when someone put his hand on my shoulders. I saw the invigilator still standing on the door chatting away with one of his colleagues. I turned around and almost froze on seeing the Head of Department sneer at me.

Minutes later, I was begging for mercy in the Director's room. A thousand apologies later, I was let off with a final warning. I was made to complete the rest of my exam in front of the prying eyes of the Director just outside his office.

After the completion of the exam, I came out. Armi was waiting outside. He was all smiles. He had done all the eight. Luck had once again failed me. I narrated him the entire story. This was one of the worst days of my life.

Nonetheless, I decided to forget the incident and start anew. Exams were finally over and time had arrived for a drinking session which Armi was so eagerly waiting for. I never developed a taste for alcohol but Armi egged me to go for it.

M.K bar wasn't very far from our hostel and very near to Sikandra, Akbar's tomb.

One man whom I could term as an ultimate drinker was Armi. After drinking he would be the fermentation tank that could release toxic gases which could contribute five percent to global warming. Living life became difficult when he drank. He could gulp down half a bottle of Vodka in one go.

We made our way inside the bar and took our seats. As usual, Armi and his Vodka became the best of friends while I sipped my quota of Vodka lime along with some *paneer pakodas.* During this period our conversation ranged from sex to the possibilities of developing a real spider-man.

All this while, the manager viewed us with suspicion as though we were some kind of dumb-headed transsexuals. Soon, Armi was off to his dream world. He kept blabbering about things which I couldn't get a hint of. I wanted to get out of the bar as soon as I could. But Armi wouldn't budge. I had to think of some idea to get him out of there.

Armi being six feet, seventy seven kilos, the idea of lifting him onto my back seemed next to impossible. So, I had no other alternative other than to shove some paneer pakodas up his nostrils. This worked instantly and he got up with a jerk all the time blabbering about some dangers and instincts which I couldn't understand. After ten minutes of bickering, he finally stepped out of the bar.

"We shouldn't go this way" Armi stammered. He just wouldn't stop blabbering.

"This is the shortest possible way to the hostel and there is nothing to fear about" I said.

No sooner had I completed the sentence, two men appeared from nowhere and confronted us. Both of them wore unusually bright cloths and seemed like some circus clowns. They were dressed in identical attires, wore large ear rings and carried two large bags. For once, I thought them to be extra-terrestrials.

"Stop" one of them said, pointing towards me.

They had sensed that Armi was drunk and I being pea sized could be their easy prey. We stopped not knowing what they were up to. One of them, short heighted, about five three took out a shiny blade like thing which I recognized to be a knife. A wave of horror gripped me. I froze and almost freaked out but Armi's pillar like physique saved me from falling down. I desperately wanted to run but being Armi's friend, I couldn't leave him alone.

"What do you want?" I asked. We were in the verge of being robbed and this was one of the silliest of questions one could have asked. Instinctively, I began taking out my watch, my wallet ready to hand it over to them.

"I want your asses" one of them barked.

"What?" I said, couldn't believe what I had just heard.

"I want your damn asses" he said.

For a moment I thought they would kick on my butt but the next moment when I saw one of them unbuttoning his pants, I almost fainted. I just couldn't believe that I was going to be raped.

"Open your pant" his voice crackled.

They wanted to rob me off my virginity. Armi looked morose. I wanted to run away but then I couldn't let them rob Armi's virginity. Friendship sucked more than anything.

Slowly, I began unbuttoning my trousers all the time praying to the heavens above to save me from the onslaught. I closed my eyes as I dropped my trousers all ready to be a sacrificial lamb.

Suddenly I heard a thud. I opened my eyes. Armi had punched the taller one right on his nose. Sensing the opportunity, I kicked the shorter one. The kick landed straight in his balls. I always followed a simple principle- when you are on the losing side, kick the balls. It was unethical but I was lucky I didn't have moral science as a subject in engineering.

He groaned in pain while the other one lay down, his nose bleeding.

"Run Armi" I screamed.

For half a kilometer, we didn't stop. I was exhausted. If it was a hundred meter dash in the Rajeeta incident, this was a marathon. I was surprised at Armi's sudden outburst. We huffed and puffed as we reached the hostel gates.

"It seems we are safe now, but how did you regain your composure?" I asked. I was puzzled.

"I wanted to teach you a lesson. Never ever doubt my instincts. When I say there is something wrong, there is" he said. I had only one conclusion. Armi could well one day become an actor.

Sadly, I never learnt the lesson.

The Confession

Fourth semester exams had already began after a one week holiday, which we spent either orkutting or playing our favorite game FIFA. Before joining engineering, biology was my favorite subject but now biology sucked more than anything. The worst part was that we had to cram ninety percent of every subject because some bloke set the question papers without knowing where the answers actually are from.

Tuesday became our favorite day, when we learnt that a very seductive damsel would take our microbiology class. Female teachers were a rarity in our college and any sighting of these species would lead to a huge hullabaloo. The first Tuesday of the fourth semester had finally arrived and I was still dreaming when I heard a loud knock on the door. My cock-a-doodle clock showed seven-thirty.

"Who is it?" I screamed.

"Armi here, open the door." He shouted back.

I opened the door only to find Armi, dressed up in gaudy attire, fully gelled hair, spiked up and ironed jeans with a combination of fully polished boots.

"Surprise...." Armi uttered with a big fat smile on his face.

It wasn't my birthday today, the results were still not out nor did I land a job yet, than what could be the reason?

"Miss Tanya is taking our first classes today..." Armi blurted.

"Oh! Gosh! Armi, you are such a sissy."

"I'll take that as a compliment, now get dressed as soon as possible. I do not want to disappoint Miss Tanya on her first class."

Brushing was as much pain as bathing or kicking the ass of the five hundred pound Big Show. I dressed as quickly as it was possible for me to do and within fifteen minutes, we were at the class.

"I can't believe I'm doing a microbiology class today." I remarked.

As usual, I selected the last row but a pull from behind stooped me.

"We are not sitting in the last bench" Armi stated in a stern voice.

"What? Have you gone crazy?"

"Yes, but we are not sitting in the last row today..."

He pulled me over to the first bench and pointed to the seat in the corner.

"We are sitting here" he said, whispering into my ears.

"This is pure torture, Armi...."

"Remember Samarth, the first impression is the last impression"

I had seen guys change when they get hooked up but guys changing because of teachers and that too, a guy like Armi, it really freaked me out. Finally the Goddess appeared and the class for the first time became silent. The first thing that caught my attention was, Armi. He was drooling. The scene instantly reminded me of the movie 'Mein Hoon Naa' where a retro Shahrukh Khan went speechless in front of the gorgeous Sushmita Sen.

I agree, she was a Goddess, had beautiful black eyes, in short a lady straight out from a 'Fair and lovely' add but she was our guru. Fifteen minutes into the class and Armi was still drooling over her. There was no respite. I sensed that he was in a reverie, maybe on a romantic get together.

"Hey, you at the corner..." a beautiful female voice sounded.

"Why are you looking at me like that? Am I some kind of an animal?

You people are good for nothing." She continued.

Armi muttered something which I guessed was 'you-are-a-wild-cat' statement.

"What? What did you say just now?" she screamed on top of her voice.

The sound of laughter ricocheted inside the classroom.

"Ma'am, Ma'am...." Armi stuttered.

"Get the hell out of my class, both of you".....she ordered.

"But Ma'am, I haven't done anything wrong" I protested.

"I said, get out of the class" Miss Goddess screamed again.

Slowly but surely, we moved out of the class amidst the row of laughter that engulfed the entire classroom. The corridor seemed longer than usual and I kicked Mr. Fatass' butt.

"You are such a dumbo"

"Sorry, Samarth, I never wanted to do that."

I could swallow everything right from raw potatoes to mashed earthworms but not insult.

"Please forgive me, Samarth...."

Armi was almost on the verge of tears which left me no other option other than squaring off.

Hunger pangs hit both of us hard and we decided to take a bite at the canteen.

"*Do samosas dijiye bhaiya*" I ordered samosas, which was the best our college could give us after assignments.

"Hey Samarth, I've got to confess something to you"

"Oh! No, not again, Armi"

Last time he didn't wash his ass after shitting and he used the same statement to tell me.

"Na, it's not what you are thinking"

"What is it then?" I asked.

"Actually I'm in love with Cobain and grunge."

"What? You aren't kidding, are you?

"No Samarth, I'm serious..."

"I'm in love with the guitar. I love Cobain playing it. I love hearing the sound of the six-string."

"Oh my God, I don't believe this, Armi?"

"You have to believe me; his songs are always on my lips these days. Your daily dose has worked magic on me."

"That's great news man...the samosa is on me."

"And I'm planning to buy a guitar soon. I have already downloaded the chords from the internet and will learn the basic steps from YouTube." Armi said, surprising me every second.

"Nice plan, but are you sure, because it's going to take a hell lot of dedication, it may even take six to seven years to master it..."

"You don't believe me, do you? Screw you....I'm leaving now....bye and Jai Kurt Cobain..." he left wishing me good bye...

"Bye Armi"

I stood still as I watched him move out of my sight. I was happy not because I implanted a part of western culture in Armi's mind but because I had implanted love and passion in him...

This confession changed the course of my life.

April fool's love

Spring finally showed its colour and Holi was a scary dream. People dressed in whites and spraying colour on each other didn't make a lot of sense. So, the best thing to do was to remain indoors. Orkut was my only friend but I didn't trust him. The reason was simple-he had found his girlfriend but I hadn't. But it was a good pastime with Armi out of sight for a couple of days. I was a Holi-phobic or whatever you would like to call. So, all doors and windows were locked and food supplies were stocked for a week because I felt that just like earthquakes, Holi had its aftershocks.

I picked up my phone and called Armi. He had gone home and was scheduled to return a week later. I dialed his number.

"Hi! thinass, what a pleasant surprise" he said.

"Shut up fatass, I didn't call you to surprise you or to wish you. I just wanted to tell you that I am enjoying my life out here and please do not call or disturb me" I said sarcastically.

"Thanks for the advice thinass but all I want to tell you is that I am returning tomorrow" he said.

"Shit, that's not very good, but if you are coming than please bring me a can of gulab jamuns" I said.

"Positive" he said.

"Thanks mate" I said and cut the line.

I checked my watch. It showed April 30, 21:30. I turned on my computer. Drives were full of crap, right from hacking tools to flash games. One could even find lingerie ads downloaded from You-tube. So, booting took an eternity. Finally, after a mind breaking wait of three minutes, Amrita Rao's sexy wallpaper cast its spell on me. Although the whole world was with me, I could feel Armi's absence. As usual, I decided on some Orkutting. I had recently joined one of the biggest communities where people played crap games and asked the crappiest of questions to each other. I hated posting answers to these questions but it was better than Armi's 'bakarchodi'.

My first post was meted by criticism by almost every member present except Shreya. Same was the case for the next post as well. Only Shreya seemed to be supporting me out of some seven lakh members in the community. That was incredulous. Taking this opportunity, I asked her if she would chat with me. The reply was positive and I invited her on G-Mail. It was Orkut's right hand and so was mine. We started chatting.

Me: Hiya, gotch you…

Shreya: Hie…

Me: So, your intro?

Shreya: read it in my profile.

I quickly brushed up through her profile. It didn't seem much impressive but I could not have said that.

Me: ya, read it…its quite impressive

I lied point-blank.

Shreya: hmmm…I am impressive.

Me: what do you do?

Shreya: studying….grad 1st year.

Me: wonderful...So, read my profile?

Shreya: yea, gone through it, nice one…

I wondered whether she was lying too.

Me: check out by blog too…actually I love writing poems.

Shreya: same here… what do you write about?

Me: love, war, relationships…

Shreya: basically, I write short quotes…

Me: oh! Is it? Tell me sum of your quotes…

Shreya: sure, but will tell you tomorrow, actually my diary is not with me and I'm too lazy to get up and search for it.

Me: not a big problem...

I was growing tired of asking questions and I wondered whether she had any questions for me.

Shreya: and what do you do?

Finally, she had a question.

Me: well I'm a rock singer and an engineering student at Guwahati...

I lied once again.

Shreya: oh! I too thought of doing engineering but physics is not my cup of tea.

Poor girl…I thought.

Me: do you listen to music?

Shreya: yea, I do.

Me: what kinds?

Shreya: it depends on my mood.

Me: did you hear about Kurt Cobain?

Shreya: yeah, I have heard many of his quotes.

A girl listening Kurt Cobain was unexpected.

Me: man, you are the first girl I've come across who likes Kurt.

Shreya: oh! Really, so you like Nirvana, and have you listened to his song 'Stay away'?

I could say that she liked pulling legs. She was intelligent too.

Me: Wow! You are amazing. I dedicate a song 'Smells like teen spirit' to you.

Shreya: lolz....

Me: Nirvana was a great band. Which is your favourite quote by the way?

Shreya: 'wanting to be someone else is a waste of the person you are'

Me: mine is 'it's better to burn out than to fade away'

Shreya: great....

Me: what else do you like?

Shreya: hmmm...I like reading novels.

Me: which ones?

Shreya: Sidney Sheldon, Morris West, Danielle Steels....

She was a prolific reader too...

Me: Sheldon is good, but Dan Brown is my favourite. I like Robert Ludlum, Michel Crichton and a bit of Salman Rushdie. They are the best contemporary writers.

Shreya: did you read Jeffery Archer?

Me: Only one of his book-Prisoner of birth.

Shreya: great....

Me: do you believe in ghosts?

Shreya: not exactly but I do believe in voodoos and all that stuff. I am pretty sure it works.

This was scary. She could be a witch or a zombie or even an extra-terrestrial.

Me: Oh! Assam is famous for voodoos.

Me: hey, can you use some spells to make me fall in love with you?

Shreya: lolz...no...Ok, I'll give it a try and I'll tell you tomorrow.

But even if you fall for me, I won't fall in for you.

Me: is it?

Shreya: actually every girl has a dream image of the guy she wants as her Mr. Perfect, and I think my Mr. Perfect is not yet born.

Me: does that mean that you're gonna marry someone 16 years younger to you?

Shreya: lolz…not so, but if I do not find my Mr. Perfect, I'm gonna marry my dad's choice.

Me: But what if I say that you've found your Mr. Perfect?

Shreya: Naa…it can't be…

Me: So, how do you expect to find your Mr. Perfect?

Shreya: left it to fate

Me: Fate; I just hate that word…tell me something about Amritsar…

Shreya: known for the golden temple, its beauty is unmatched…

Me: yeah, beautiful Amritsar, beautiful golden temple, beautiful Shreya!!

I realized how good a flirt I was.

Shreya: lolz…who said I'm beautiful...

Me: You must be beautiful…for sure…

Shreya: Do you have a chick at hand?

Me: Yeah! I do have one..,

Shreya: May I know her name if you don't mind?

Me: Shreya…lolz…

Shreya: lolz…

Me: Jokes apart, I had a crush on a girl today…

Shreya: hmmmm…..which girl?

Me: Shreya again…

Shreya: Lolz…stop kidding…

Me: On a serious note, I dreamt about a girl yesterday

Shreya: That's certainly not me....coz I never met you yesterday...

Me: Wrong again! It's you...it's five past twelve midnight!

Shreya: lolz....you have got good humour!

Me: thanks for the compliment!

Shreya: You are such a kidoo...

Me: Kidoo? Does that mean future boyfriend?

I was a genius, a terrific flirt. I thought I could someday become a Casanova.

Shreya: lolzzz...no!

Me: Peace!

Shreya: you live in Assam na..?

Me: yea, Guwahati to be precise. I was brought up at Shillong. Heard of Shillong?

Shreya: yup, heard about the beautiful landscape there

Me: Shillong is also known as the Scotland of the East...It's as beautiful as Scotland itself.

Shreya: My folks basically hail from Darjeeling.

Me: Another great hill station!

Shreya: Are u a veggie?

Me: I hate vegetables but I'll start loving it if I start loving Shreya...

Shreya: What time is it?

Me: Gosh! It's late...2:36 to be precise...and I have a Fluid Flow test tomorrow.

Shreya: Don't worry you will rock the test...

Me: only if you help me with your voodoo...

Shreya: What's your height by the way?

Me: I hope you don't like short people because I'm 170 cms...

Shreya: I do not dislike them either…but I'm 172 cms…

Me: Definitely, I'm not going to appear for the test…I would rather go for a height increment therapy…

Shreya: lolz…sleep heartily boy…and do your test well…

Me: I guess it's late…it was nice talking to you...

Shreya: Same here…will you be online tomorrow?

Me: Definitely…see you tomorrow…bye, tc...

Shreya: bye…

I turned off the computer. Butterflies were already flying inside my stomach. I always wanted to have a girlfriend as intelligent as Shreya. Beauty did matter what mattered more was brains and she had plenty of that.

I checked out my watch. It was fifteen past three. I decided it was time to sleep.

A loud knock on the door woke me up. I checked out my watch. It showed 8:30. I fifteen minutes I had to reach college. I got out of my bed and opened the door. Armi stood there. The devil had finally arrived.

"We have a test today, don't we?" he said.

"Welcome back to test-land" I said, still feeling drowsy.

In fifteen minutes we were in the classroom. I had studied nothing and Shreya flashed in and out of my mind. The invigilator distributed the papers. The questions were incomprehensible but I had to write something.

Kurt Cobain came to my rescue. To prolong my answers, I added some Nirvana lyrics. I was the best at it and I could have done nothing more.

After the test, Armi came up to me.

"It seems like you have rocked the test" he said.

"I have for certain" I said.

"How was your Holi?" he said, as I saw him give dirty looks to one of his ex-crushes.

"I think I'm in love" I said.

"With Holi…?" he said, bemused by my answer.

"With Shreya" I said.

"And who's this Shreya" he asked.

"There's this sweet little girl from Amritsar whom I met yesterday online" I said. Armi strained his ears such that it almost reached my mouth. He was more than a keen listener.

"She's intelligent, funny and beautiful" I said.

"April fool's Love, huh?" he said.

"Seems so, but it's too early to predict" I said.

"I hope you are not being fooled" he said.

"I'm sure I'm the wisest April fool you'll find around" I said.

We came out of the campus and headed straight towards the hostel.

"I'm tired and I need some rest. See you later" I said, as I entered my room and closed the door behind.

I quickly turned on my computer and waited for Shreya. My Orkut heading said 'Grunge or Die'. For two hours, I sat beside the computer looking at the empty screen waiting for her. After a torturous two and a half hour wait she arrived. I quickly opened the chat window and began.

Me: Hi! How was your night?

Shreya: I didn't sleep…the entire night, I read a novel.

Me: Which one?

Shreya: Naked Face by Sidney Sheldon…

Me: All Sheldons are fantastic…

Shreya: they sure are…

Me: I was listening to 'Sajni' by Jal…cool song…

Shreya: Then sing it for me…

Me: Na…naa…my Hindi diction is pretty bad…

Shreya: You got to sing it for me…

The fact was that I had only heard of the song by its name. I was in a fix. I just wanted to continue the conversation but I never expected that she would ask me to sing it for her.

Me: Any alternatives?

Shreya: Sajni, Sajni and Sajni…

I turned on the microphone. I had to find a solution. After all, I was a genius. I quickly opened You-Tube played and the song in a low volume. I quickly opened another site which contained the lyrics and I began. At the end of the rendition she clapped. I had pulled off a miracle. No doubt, I was a genius.

Shreya: You have a wonderful voice…

Me: And you have the sweetest voice I have ever heard.

This time I wasn't lying. Even nightingales would have been ashamed if she had been around. My heart skipped a beat as I listened to her.

Shreya: I can't talk on the microphone much….didi's around…

Me: it's fine…and now that I've sung a song for you, can I accept you as my gf?

Shreya: lolz…let's be friends…

Me: Gf means g-mail friend…

I had intentionally asked her and it was worth a try.

Shreya: Shit! I forgot I had my coaching classes…I need to go…

Me: When will you be online next?

Shreya: I'll be waiting for you at night…

With a heavy heart, I closed the chat window. I had to wait for another four hours before she would return. I felt more butterflies fly in my stomach. Love was definitely in the air. I was tired and I dozed off.

I was still sleeping till I heard a loud knock on the door. I checked out my cock-a-doodle watch. It showed 10:05 P.M. I thought that the devil had arrived. But to my utter surprise, I found one of my seniors standing, holding a huge bag.

"Samarth, I've got some work for you" he said, as he entered inside my room.

Shreya would be waiting for me and I couldn't refuse my senior. I had to oblige. I couldn't tell him I was in love either.

"I've got three assignments which you need to complete for me tonight" he said. I loathed him.

I had to think of some idea to get rid of him. I picked up my phone and messaged Armi.

"Here, take these…it will take an hour or two" he said as he handed me a pile of files.

"Sir, what do you think about ghosts?" I said as I went through the files.

"There's nothing called ghosts…these are all imaginations, but why are you asking that?" he said.

"I sometimes feel someone moving around here…a woman in fact" I said.

"It's nothing but a hypothesis created by your mind" he said.

Suddenly, the lights went off. Armi had switched off the main power supply.

"Seems like there's a power cut" he said.

"I don't think so…what was that?" I said, pointing towards the door.

Armi had wrapped one of his bed sheets and ran along the balcony and disappeared in a flash such that he was visible for only a second.

"Oh-my-God…I just saw something" he said.

"That was what I was taking about…I see it every full moon night" I added.

"Let me check out" he said as he stepped outside.

I feared that Armi would get caught and so to divert the attention I screamed aloud.

"What happened?" he said, as he came rushing inside the room. I lay on the floor pretending to writhe in pain. I clenched my teeth and curled my body like a cobra.

"Oh-my-God" he said. From the corner of my eyes, I saw him pick up his bag and dash out like a mad man. The trick worked and Armi switched on the lights once again. Armi entered the room and we hi-fived with each other.

"He would never come back again" Armi said.

As I danced around the room, my eyes fell on a familiar figure standing right at the door. It was the senior. I stood still, ashamed at what I had done. Armi slipped out wishing me goodbye.

"That was nice, but I'm your senior" he said. I remained silent.

"You could have told me that you didn't want me here" ha said.

"I'm sorry, Sir" I stammered.

"Hurt someone and then ask for forgiveness" he said.

"I'll never come back again" he said and left.

A minute later, Armi came back again. He shut the door and started dancing. I danced along with him. We were shameless drudgers.

I got back on the computer and waited. It was almost eleven and

Shreya had still not arrived. I waited for two long hours until I dozed off sitting on the chair itself.

A loud buzz woke me up. I quickly opened the chat window. It was Shreya.

Me: What are you doing at this hour of the night?

Shreya: I've been buzzing you since the last half an hour…

Me: You are crazy…

Shreya: I'll take that as a compliment…

Me: Can I talk to you?

Shreya: didi's sleeping…anyways note down my number.

I noted down her number as fast as I could.

Me: When do I call you?

Shreya: Anytime after noon…

Me: Sure…

Shreya: I just checked out your blog…You write beautiful poems…

Me: Thanks…

Shreya: Write one for me…

Me: I'm a nerd in writing romantic poems…

Shreya: You have to…

Me: I'll give it a shot…

Shreya: I've to go now lest I get caught…

Me: I will definitely give you a call tomorrow…

Shreya: I'll wait…

Me: Bye, tc

Shreya: Bye…

I turned off my computer. I realized that the girl had fallen for me. So had I. It was definitely love. I dozed off again.

I had a huge task at hand. I had never written a romantic poem and my sixth attempt had proved to be futile. I had to surprise her in an hour.

Finally, in the eighth attempt, I wrote 'Ode to Love'. It was a masterpiece. I posted it in my blog.

As soon as the clock struck twelve, I picked up my phone and called her.

"Hi Samarth" the sweetest voice on earth responded.

"Hi Shreya...before I say anything, check out my blog" I said.

She returned back in a minute.

"I still can't believe you did it...it's wonderful...in fact it's the most beautiful piece of composition I've ever read" she said. She sounded exuberant.

"I told you, I'm a genius" I said.

"Thank you so much, can I read it for you?" she said.

"The poem's yours..." I said.

Ode to Love

From the depth of seashore,
where the waves roar
Down she came with a majestic smile,
couldn't hold myself, I stood a while.
She made my heart stumble
and I just turned so humble,
all I can just make her feel
yes I LOVE YOU with zeal.
She made me dream and,
made me adore,

for all that I allure.
She is just like FREYA
and this poem is for the beautiful
SHREYA'.

She read the poem aloud and I realized that destiny was carving a way for itself. In just a short while, two souls who till the other day never knew each other, were now united.

Days rolled on till the 23rd of April when I finally decided to bare my heart. I called her up.

"Hi Shreya" I said.

"Hi Samarth…thanks for calling…actually I'm moving out with my parents for a couple of days" she said.

"What? Where? Why?" I said. I couldn't have asked more questions.

"I'm going to Shimla for a week" she said.

"For a week..?" I said.

"I'll call you once I return…oh…didi is here…I have to go now…bye"

Before I could say anything more, she cut the line. I was dejected. The universe always conspired against me whenever I wanted its support. I had planned to say so many things. Now, I had to wait for another week.

I was in love and Armi thought he was too.

"I have a crush on that girl" he said, pointing to a bespectacled twenty something girl who waved at him. Armi waved at her in return.

"Isn't she hot?" he said.

"I really don't think so" I said.

"Actually, I was just kidding…how can she be my girlfriend...?"

Armi said. He made a complete u-turn from his previous statement. For Armi, the hotness quotient mattered the most. He was despised by almost all the girls of our class.

"I'm missing her loads" I said.

"Ah! Ha, lover boy…you are definitely in love" he said.

"Thanks for your analysis" I said. I left him alone and returned back to the hostel. Shreya's voice echoed inside my mind every time I thought about her.

A week later, Shreya called. Hurriedly, I picked up her call.

"I'm back" she said.

Her sweet voice acted like a drug and calmed me down. My heart was getting heavier by the day and I decided not to wait any longer.

"I've got something to tell you" I said.

"What is it Samarth?" she said. I crossed my fingers.

"I think I'm in love with you" I said. No reply came from the other side. I feared for the worst.

"Believe me…I'm not lying, I missed you when you were gone" I said. There was still no reply.

"I already have a boyfriend" she said, after seven agonizing seconds. I almost broke down on hearing this. I remained silent.

"Wouldn't you like to know his name?" she asked.

"Na…na…tell" I stammered.

"Samarth Dasgupta" she said.

I jumped up in the air and screamed as loud as I could. Armi rushed inside my room.

"Are you all right?" he said.

"I'm in seventh heaven" I said and hugged him tight.

Two souls, a thousand kilometers from each other and yet united, it was nothing short of a miracle. I couldn't have asked for more. I thanked the Lord for giving me the most prized possession of my life.

The Golden Sojourn

Life was never the same after Shreya came from nowhere. She was hard to understand yet I loved her. She was a complexity but life had already changed and I could not stop myself from loving her more. I had written quite a few poems on war and violence but romantic poems were never my cup of tea until I wrote 'Ode to love'. That was when I discovered my talent of writing romantic poems.

Fourth semester exams were knocking at the door. Like always, exams were the worst nightmare. Preparation for the fourth was nil and backlogs were piling up like dust on government files. Even worse, I had exchanged two of my course books for three game DVD's.

Shreya was eager to meet me and I made up my mind to visit Amritsar. I was hugely excited at the prospect but exams were posing to be a hurdle on my way.

Three days prior to the commencement of the examination, Armi came running into my room.

"There's a huge problem" he said. He was completely out of breath.

"What happened?" I asked.

"Do you know the guy Vijay?" he said.

"Vijay, the one who is accused of rioting and hooliganism" I said.

"Rioting, hooliganism and a double murder" he added.

"What happened to him?" I asked.

"He was pulling my leg and I thrashed him in the middle of *Khandari chowk"* he said.

"What the hell? I said. Armi had just thrashed the most wanted criminal in Agra.

"I never knew he was Vijay. It was after the thrashing that I came to know about it" he explained.

"You are dead. They will find you out, skin you and burn you alive" I said, enjoying every bit of the drama that was unfolding.

"Stop this nonsense. We have to get out of here as soon as possible for a day or two" he said.

"Not we, you should get out of Agra as soon as possible" I said.

"Actually, they know me as Samarth Dasgupta" he said, flashing a wicked smile.

"You bloody rascal" I shouted.

There was no way I could have stayed here in Agra. Now, the guys were after Samarth Dasgupta. Those guys were hardcore criminals and I didn't want myself to get skinned.

"I've go a brilliant idea" I said.

"Let's visit Amritsar for a day or two. That way, we can be safe and I can meet Shreya" I said.

"Brilliant idea… Let's pack our bags and get moving. They can be here anytime now" Armi said, as he returned back to his room.

Airlines were unaffordable, even the low cost ones so trains were the next best option. I packed my bag. I was ready, ready for a golden journey to meet a golden girl.

"Hey Armi, take a pair of bed sheets with you but I hope we don't need them" I said.

"Sure Samarth, I understand" he said.

As soon as I finished my packing my stuff, Armi rushed into my room.

"I think they are here. We better get out of here" he said, as he locked the door of my room from inside. I peeped out through the keyhole. The sight sent down shivers down my spine. There were more than twenty five guys armed with knuckles, belts and baseball bats. They had choked our escape route.

"Quickly, through that window" I said, pointing to a small window which led down to the hostel backyard. Armi quickly opened the window and began climbing down the thin sanitary pipe. It was my turn. I was terrified of heights but I managed to keep my cool. Half the climb was completed when my feet got entangled in one of the wires and I fell down with a thud, head first. Armi picked me up, carried me on his shoulders and ran as first as he could. He flung me across the wall and I landed on the other side, head first again. Armi jumped over the wall without a scratch.

My head swelled up like a balloon.

"Sorry Samarth, I guess we are safe now" he said. I was crossed with him.

"How dare you fling me?" I screamed at him. My head hurt but we had a narrow escape.

We brought two tickets. The train was teeming with people. I doubted if we would get a berth. But there was still hope. Bribe could get you anything in this world. There was little time left and Armi and I began a frantic search for the TTE but he seemed nowhere in sight.

As time passed, my heart beat faster. Five minutes before departure, the devil in the black dress appeared. We hurried towards him.

"Sir, I want two berths" Armi said politely.

"I can't give you any" the TTE said.

"But sir, we'll pay for it" I said.

"What? You think you can bribe me. Do you know who I'm? I'm an honest man. I will have you and your cockroach arrested" he screamed on top of his voice.

"Ok…ok…Sir, I'm really sorry for offending you" I said. I thought of him to be a fucking egotist.

"What do we do now?" Armi asked.

"Bed sheets" I said, winking at him.

The train started moving albeit at a snail's pace and we climbed into one of the relatively empty bogies.

Our primary job was to find a suitable place where we could lay our asses. The train was immensely crowded. The festive season was just round the corner and hordes of pilgrims from all over India were pouring in to Amritsar. After an intense search, we discovered an empty place just adjacent to the train toilets. We placed the bed sheets on the floor and spread out.

I cursed the train driver incessantly for making the journey seem like a never ending experience. It was a twelve hour long journey and I hadn't told Shreya about my visit yet. I had planned a surprise. One more night, and my love would be with me.

Armi, meanwhile, dozed off and I was left wondering about the past few years during which my life changed considerably.

The stinking toilet coupled with Armi's snoring made it impossible for me to sleep. I decided to write something. Ten minutes passed but I couldn't get any idea.

"Mauje le lo….Mauje" the voice called out.

I looked up. A beautiful sight greeted me. I had never seen a woman as beautiful as her. She carried with her a bagful of socks. I was mesmerized by her beauty. Armi had certainly missed what I would call as the eighth wonder of the world.

An idea struck me. I decided to dedicate my next poem to the shocking beauty. I had finally found something to write and jotted down a poem titled 'The S(h)ocking Beauty.

Miles of iron strips, underneath my feet,
Rolling wheels, sound erupting from beneath,
Strange faces gazing everywhere,
Smell of sweat filled the air

La Belle, she came,
with a bagful of socks she played a game,
A game which I could never understand
never in my life I had a feeling so grand

My sorrow it went up in smoke,
In matter of minutes I got soaked
in drops of joy and as I closed my eyes,
all my pain eased deep inside

As she moved on,
I stood still, as I watched her gone
my sojourn had come to an end,
Was the Shocking beauty Godsend???

It mainly took me an hour to jot down the sixteen odd lines but it was worth writing for the shocking beauty.

Armi was sleeping like a log but I was too excited to sleep or eat anything. Three hours passed, the date changed and sleep crept into my eyes.

I woke up late in the morning. Armi was standing at the door puffing away. This was his breakfast.

"Good morning Armi" I said.

"Good morning thinass" he wished me back.

"Where are we?" I asked.

"We are about to reach Amritsar" he said.

It was a long journey and as the first sights of Amritsar greeted us I felt elated. I called up Shreya.

"Would you like to meet me today?" I said.

"What? Are you crazy? Don't tell me you are at Amritsar" she said. I heard a loud crashing sound come from the other side of the phone. Apparently, she jumped off her bed on hearing me and in the process broke a priceless piece of artifact.

"A pleasant surprise for you honey" I said.

"Wow! I can't believe this" she said. She was exuberant.

"Where do we meet by the way" I asked.

"I'll call you after my class gets over" she said.

I cut the line after I received a bountiful of kisses. This was the day I was waiting for three months.

The train came to a screeching halt and we put our first steps in the golden city.

Shreya had promised me to call after her class but the prolonged wait was killing me. We took a hotel adjacent to the Jallianwala Bagh and the Golden temple being barely two hundred meters away.

Fortunately, the hotel had a cabin empty we gleefully accepted the keys to the double bedroom.

As I looked through the window, a colourful sight greeted me. Hundreds of people, all dressed in garish attires and colourful turbans moved in the same direction- in the direction of the Golden temple.

I was eagerly waiting for Shreya's call.

"Do you know what a punk means?" I asked Armi.

"I guess it means idiot, moron, jerk..." he said.

"Punk means Samarth. Samarth and punk are synonymous" I said. Armi laughed aloud.

"If you are a punk than I'm a baby kangaroo" he said. He just couldn't stop laughing.

It was true. With headgears, bracelets and skull lockets I resembled a punk. In college, my fellow mates called me 'spikey' because of my spiked hair. I enjoyed being showered all the attention.

This time I decided to wear formal attire. A simple plain jeans and a T-shirt was what I opted for. It was my first date and I had to look beautiful.

"Armi get a quick shower. You are stinking like a skunk" I said.

"Shut up and do your own job" he shot back.

Shreya finally called me up.

"Are you ready" she asked.

"All ready to meet you, my love" I said.

"Reach Renjith Avenue in twenty minutes, I'll be there" she said.

"Okay honey, see you" I said and cut the line. I told Armi about my plans. I invited him to join me on my first date but he refused. He wanted to check out some Punjabi *kudis* but ditched the idea later when he saw a girl bashing up a boy in the middle of the street. After five minutes of bickering, he finally relented. We came out of the hotel.

There were neither cabs nor buses. We took a rickshaw. It moved at a snails pace and after twenty minutes of an agonizing journey through road full of potholes, Renjith Avenue beckoned. Armi jumped off the rickshaw. Apparently, he was more excited than I was.

I looked around but she seemed nowhere in sight. All I could see were the large departmental stores and swanky restaurants. I called her up again.

"I've reached here. Where are you?" I said.

"I'm on my way" she said.

I checked out my watch. It showed 1:30 P.M. Pangs of hunger struck me. As I waited near the 'Yellow Chili', a silver coloured Indica stopped beside me.

Out came Shreya. As my eyes fell upon her, my heart screamed out in delight. She looked beautiful. She was dressed in a black satin top and blue jeans. She had beautiful brown eyes and I couldn't stop myself from drooling.

The weather was hot and humid and she came like a breath of fresh air. She had black flowing hair and her face resembled an innocent kid with a tint of naughtiness in them.

A small pimple popped out from her left cheek but that made her look all the more startling.

"Hi, *roshogolla*" I said, as she stepped out of the car.

"Hi, Samarth" she said and smiled as she came towards me.

"Where do we go from here? I'm feeling hungry" I said.

"Come with me" she said as she led us to her car. I turned around to call Armi. He had disappeared.

"Armi doo, where are you?" I called out.

Armi appeared. He had hidden himself behind a parked car.

"This is Armaan" I said, as I introduced the two to each other.

Inside the car, I sat beside Shreya while Armi sat at the back. As she drove, I stole occasional glances at her. Adrenaline flowed in my blood and I felt a tremendous urge to kiss her. But the devil was sitting at the back and I felt he was watching my actions and reactions the whole time.

She had put on some weight but that made her look even better and here I was- a forty-kilo moron dating a fifty kilo belle. We were not the perfect couple but shared the perfect love.

"Where are we going?" I said.

"El-dorado" she answered.

"What about the Fiji islands?" I said. She smiled.

"What about heaven?" she said, winking at me. Armi laughed aloud.

"How was your journey by the way?" she asked.

"Fantastic, except for the fact that we spent the entire night sleeping beside the stinking toilet" I said.

"Great" she said.

She stopped the car by the side of a small restaurant named El-dorado.

The restaurant was spruced up and the relaxed ambience was much refreshing. Most importantly, the crowd was much less than I had anticipated. The restaurant was dimly lit and Kenny G's instrumentals acted like weed. In short, El-dorado was Eden.

We took the table right at the centre. I sat beside her while Armi sat opposite to me. Shreya's face reflected the very faint light that illuminated the Eden. I could smell her perfume that she had put on. It was more than intoxicating.

"Samarth and Armaan, order anything you want" she said.

Still I had to make an offer.

"I'll order, let me have a look at the menu" I said.

The menu had everything in it, right from pasta to sushi. I hated Japanese and Italian cuisines and I left it to Shreya to decide.

She ordered pizzas, vegetable bullets and some sophisticated drinks with sophisticated names, which I do not have enough neurons to remember.

"I've something for you" she said.

She had the sweetest voice, I ever heard. I watched in awe as she opened her bag, took out a card and handed it to me. I was dumbstruck. She had made the card herself. I opened the card and began reading it. It couldn't have been better than this. She had written my own poem 'Ode to love'. My face lighted up and I could feel her love for me. Life had become so beautiful.

It was my turn but I felt ashamed when I presented to her the card I had brought for her. Her incredible artistic ability eclipsed mine.

"Thank you so much, I've something more for you" she said. I wondered what other surprises she had in store for me.

She opened her bag, took out a Dan Brown and presented it to me.

"Read the book after you reach home" she said. I wondered what was inside it.

Fortunately, I had a Paulo Coelho with me and I gifted it to her. The day was saved.

Feasting over, we decided for some sightseeing. This time Armi decided against coming with us but Shreya wouldn't let him roam alone.

As we came out of the restaurant, two guys confronted us.

"I want to talk to her" one of them said to me. I was terrified.

I held Shreya's hand and led her towards the car. The guys trailed us.

"Let me handle this" Shreya said. I was bewildered.

"No, you aren't doing anything" I said, shaking my head.

We got inside the car. The guys just wouldn't leave. They blocked our way.

"Drive your car over us madam" I heard one of them say. Shreya was furious. She started the car and accelerated. I thought the guys were dead until she stepped on the brakes just at the right time. The guys ran for their lives. Shreya had a good laugh. I looked at her bemused. I was stunned by her act.

"I know how to handle such guys" she said.

If Armi was a tiger, Shreya was a lioness. I was surely a lamb.

Armi struck to his word of leaving the two of us alone and we dropped him at a small distance from the hotel.

"You look beautiful" I said, as soon as Armi left.

I couldn't stop myself. She smiled and her face glowed. She was doing a great job- driving without bumping into the numerous potholes on the road and tackling the self proclaimed versatile artist of the century.

"I've something more for you" she said.

"I didn't know that you are a gift factory" I said.

"Actually I'm a warehouse" she said. I nodded.

Once again, she opened her bag, took out a small gift package and handed it to me.

"Should I open it now or after reaching home" I asked.

"Open it now" she said.

I opened the package. The sight was breathtaking. A crystal heart lay inside. It was the most beautiful gift I had ever received.

"I've never received a gift as beautiful as this" I said, as I looked at the crystal.

"Nor will you ever" she said

I caressed her silky-smooth hair and clutched her hand tightly. Although, I was a wannabe romantic, I was doing pretty well. I looked into her eyes. She was definitely the girl of my dreams. I slowly moved forward and kissed on her glowing cheeks.

"Love is beautiful" she said.

"And so is life" I said. She nodded.

"When will you return?" she said.

"I'm going nowhere" I said.

I moved forward and kissed on her lips. She blushed and I could only savour the moment.

"I've written something for you" I said. I took out a piece of paper and read aloud a poem which I had written for her. The poem was titled 'When I held your hand'.

When I held your hand ,the sun shined
Murky waters glistened, I was overjoyed,
Ecstasy crept in ,nothing else mattered,
Still remember the day, I was in tears

When I held your hand, our hearts came closer
In your mystifying eyes, I helplessly wandered
and as I danced to the tunes of love,
there were moments I truly savoured

When I held your hand, I said a silent prayer,
that we would be together and together, forever
You gave me a reason to smile,
Enriched my life and made it worthwhile

And as I still hold your hand
and walk over the golden sand,
I make a promise, Shreya ,I'll hold your hand
and walk a thousand miles till the end....

She clutched my hands tightly.

"I would never let you go" she said.

"Nor would I" I said.

I just had Shreya in my mind. It was an eventful day and one of the best days of my life.

It was getting late. Shreya dropped me near the hotel. With a heavy heart, I bade goodbye and went inside. I would always treasure this day. As soon as I entered the room, Armi shouted.

"Let's celebrate this day, thinass" he said. Celebration meant alcohol.

"I'm not drinking tonight" I said.

"But I'm" he said. He took out a bottle of Vodka from his bag and I came out of the room. A visit to Amritsar would be incomplete without a visit to the Golden Temple. I quickly made my way through the massive crowd and entered inside the temple.

As I queued up, I looked at the sky. It was dotted with innumerable stars and for the first time I was mesmerized by its beauty. Love is surely the purest feeling.

As I entered inside the temple, I threw myself at the altar and prayed. I prayed for Shreya and I prayed for my dreams.

I returned back to the hotel only to find Armi guzzling down another bottle of Vodka.

"Bloody drunkard" I said to myself.

"We have a train to catch tomorrow" I said.

"I'm going nowhere. Alcohol here cost half of what it does in Agra" he said. I decided to remain silent.

As I lay on the bed, I received a message. It read-

Chk out da mail I sent u

Urgent..

It was Shreya. She had more surprises in store for me. I quickly rushed out to an internet café and checked out the mail. My heart leapt up in joy as I read a poem she had written for me.

I miss those moments spent together,
under the shades of BARISTA in not so pleasant weather.
I miss those hands that held me tight,
and the way they guide me to the right.
I miss those car rides,
with you looking at me from the side.

I miss that kiss,
which was just a mere touch of lips.
I miss that "BABY",
which you used to call me like a lady.
I miss that time,
when you held my hand and told me, "YOU ARE MINE"

I have tried to pour my heart out,
With this little poem which speaks volumes of what you are about.
I am sorry if I disappointed you in any way,
But truly I've prayed for you to always be happy and gay
I know its getting a bit bigger,
May be I should stop before you pull on the trigger.
Last but not the least
even if world ceases to exist,

I LOVE YOU...n I always will!

I messaged her back.

Thanx, it's better than 'Ode to love'
Luv u.

This was the most special day of my life. I returned back to the hotel. Armi had already fallen asleep. I was tired too. I lay down and within minutes, I dozed off.

The Sardar Unplugged

I was ecstatic. Life had never been so philanthropic before. It seemed my life was complete. But still I had many questions left unanswered. Will all my dreams come true?

I had called up Jerry twice after we first met but couldn't figure out dates for a meet up. He was busy with his job and I was busy with my semester exams.

At the crack of dawn, Armi woke me up. The time had come for us to leave Amritsar. I called up Shreya and bade her goodbye for the last time. Everything that was happening seemed to be a mere con-incidence. Everything seemed to be happening by chance. Fate was making a road for itself.

Luckily, this time around we got berths and Armi as usual began his fight with me for the window seat. He had this little kid in him who sometimes popped out of the blue and I enjoyed every bit of his insanity. The train wasn't much crowded and analyzing the situation I figured out that the journey back to Agra would be much less an adventurous ordeal.

Four other passengers sat besides us in our compartment. A couple sat with their little son, his face grim with grief reminding me of the first day of my schooling when I was terrified and agonized by the endless wails erupting from my classroom. Of course, I didn't cry. I was a brave hearted child having undergone a traumatic childhood myself.

I never told my story to anyone and kept it hidden it the farthest corner of my heart. The sullen face of the child took me fourteen years back to Shillong. I decided it was time I unravel my story to Armi who now had become my best friend.

"Would you like to hear a story?" I asked Armi.

"I love tales" he said. I began.

Shillong, 1992:

Shillong is also known as the Scotland of the East for its majestic beauty. My father grew up in a tiny neighborhood of Malki. Set amidst the picturesque hills and the pine trees, its beauty was unmatched.

Trouble started brewing up in the year 1991 and the condition worsened in the year 1992. The Khasis were the natives of Meghalaya and they wanted the non-tribals' who had settled their in large numbers to leave their state. When a peaceful protest failed, the Khasis decided to go for a violent agitation.

August 3, 1992

I was four years old and didn't have any idea what was going on. My father was a popular figure among the locals and had a lot of good Khasi friends. Tension was simmering among some locals. They thought that my father had influenced many of their friends to stay away from the agitation. Our neighbor was also a Khasi but we shared cordial relations with him.

At about 8:30 in the morning on that fateful day, our neighbor rushed in to our home. He informed my father that some locals had prepared a hit list and dad was at the top of the list. They had planned to wipe out our entire family. Our neighbor had already made plans to help us escape.

Our destination was the CPWD quarters. To reach there we had to cross a small stream and climb a hill at a small distance from our home.

My father refused. He wouldn't leave his home. He would rather die than become a refugee. He stood like a rock and decided to stay back. Night crept in slowly and we put off all the lights just in order to confuse the rioters. Our home was surrounded on all sides by huge walls and that couldn't be scaled easily.

The clock struck ten and a loud bang in the main game alarmed us. My father peeped in through the window and in the darkness and mist; he saw shadows armed with daggers, knives and swords.

Dad returned and we huddled up together. We could only pray and hope that God would somehow save us from this onslaught.

There were around twenty people shouting slogans and swearing to kill each and every non-tribal that dwelled in the locality. My father picked up the phone and dialed the emergency number but after a minute's beep the phone went dead. We were totally cut-off.

Suddenly, the atmosphere grew silent. War cries had stopped. I could only hear the chirping of the crickets and the sound of the swaying pine trees. Lightning streaked across the sky heralding the arrival of rain. I thought the rain God's had smiled on us.

"Is that really true? I mean, you never told me about that before" Armi interrupted me in between.

"Everything that I'm saying is absolutely true" I said.

"What happened after that" Armi said.

"Now that you have interrupted me, let's take a coffee break" I said, as I ordered two cups of coffee.

As I narrated Armi the story of my life, my eyes fell on a young Sardar who was listening intently to me. He had bright blue eyes and his turban complemented the colour of his eyes. He wore a white shirt and black trousers with finely polished shoes and looked like a young businessman to me. He was tall and handsome; almost the same height as Armi but the most striking feature was his face. He seemed less a Sardar and more a north-easterner although I rubbished my hypothesis moments later thinking that somehow I had lost my sanity. But there was a mystery surrounding him. That curiosity gave me goose bumps in my tummy.

"Hey thinass, I want to know more about what happened on that fateful night" Armi said. He had guzzled his cup of coffee in precisely a minute.

Seeing Armi's eagerness, I decided to continue with my story.

My father looked out through the window but this time he couldn't see anyone. I couldn't understand anything and so kept staring at my mother all the time. The night seemed longer than usual and the burning candles threw up ghastly shadows on the walls. Time seemed to have stopped and dad continued to check out the doors every now and then. No wonders the rioters could have sneaked in through the back door but there weren't any attempts yet. The whole night, my father spent guarding our home.

"Did anything happen that night?" Armi asked me.

"Questions later Armi, first let me complete my story" I shot back.

The next day when I woke, I found my father sitting in the drawing room along with our neighbor. I couldn't understand what they were discussing but dad's dismal look said it all. He finally decided to leave. There was no other option. His family was in danger. He finally gave up. Poignant agony was visible on his face. Tears rolled down his cheeks as he said something to mama. We had to leave home, maybe forever.

Mama packed our bags. Dad packed his radio and his antique gramophone along with some records. He had a fascination for gramophones.

Curfew had been imposed by the government that day and police van patrolled the streets. The PWD quarters situated on the hill top was our destination since the quarters were considered to be a safe heaven.

Finally, we readied to leave home. As my father put the final lock on the door, his face swelled up with grief. We could only hope that someday we would return back and live life like we had done before. I could notice the pain on his face. Our neighbor decided to accompany us. We tiptoed through a tiny opening on the backyard wall as we passed our bags to one another.

The stream carried with it little water and it was not the toughest job in the world cross. The toughest job, in fact, was to leave our ancestral home and see it standing alone without a support.

As we began crossing the stream, we heard two shots. Bullets whizzed past our ears. It missed my dad by a whisker. My dad froze, unable to move any longer but mom egged him to carry on.

More shots were fired. We had crossed the stream by then and dad shouted to us to take cover behind some trees. Moments later, we heard police sirens. More shots were fired which lasted for about five minutes or I thought so because time had stopped ticking. Everything fell silent. We resumed our journey. We moved out of the thick foliage and made our way through the narrow pathway which the washer men used to climb downhill. After twenty minutes of a zigzag climb, we safely reached our destination.

"In the end, you reached safely, isn't it? Armi asked.

"Yeah, we did" I said.

"What happened after that? Did you return?" Armi said.

Curfew was relaxed after a few days and dad decided that we leave Shillong forever. Normalcy didn't return and the situation was quite tense. A week later, we shifted to a new location and after a month we shifted to Guwahati. That's how we arrived at Guwahati.

"I understand the pain of leaving home" Armi said with a shrug.

"Those memories still haunt me" I said.

"Sad enough but now you are enjoying your life like never before. Life has paid you back everything" he said, trying to be cheerful.

"Yeah, it has, but sometimes those memories haunt me. Like today, when he brought back to me reminiscences of those days" I said, pointing to the kid who was now playing gleefully without a hint of the pain which he expressed before.

"Come on, cheer up now. I've got an idea" he said.

"What idea?" I said.

"Let's write a song based on the incidents which you have just narrated" he said.

"Great idea" I said.

As I looked around, I saw the young Sardar sitting with his eyes closed. He was meditating or I thought so. I could see tension on his face. I could not read his mind and I wanted to do so, badly, and for the first time in my life I wished I was a psychic. I took a pen and a paper and began writing down the first few lines of a very gripping poem titled 'Violence'.

There's a boy whose story you would want to know
fucking crazy his life, it was not a show
Violence all his life was what he saw
Grew up between guns and bombs, not any see-saw
At six he left the city with his family
Wandered around like a refugee
with just two bags and a suitcase,
how far could they go???
And then came the bolt from the blue
A bomb ripped up his dad, he had no clue
The boy grew up, till he was eighteen
Blood in his eyes, he wanted to kill'em

Revenge was what he lived for
He wanted to kill his father's tormentor
For Gods sake please stop the violence
Because it kills the innocence
Save the world, I shout to the heavens
Why have I been forsaken???
I feel like I'm having an aneurysm
I slash my wrists, God damn
Time stands still as I loose my soul
Was this my ultimate goal??

With Armi's help, I completed the entire poem in just under an hour. The poem was even more gripping than my life.

Every time I looked at the young Sardar, my gut told me that there was something wrong with him. There was something hidden behind those blue eyes. I decided to take the lead and talk to him.

"Hi! I'm Samarth" I said, introducing myself and forwarded my hands.

"Hello, I'm Mriganka" the Sardar introduced himself. The name sounded purely north-easterner.

"I'm an engineering student at Agra. I belong to Guwahati. What do you do?" I said.

"Then you can call me Mriganka Saikia or Mig" he said, after a brief pause.

I was shell shocked. He was an Assamese and a north-easterner after all. My gut was right. We shook hands but I didn't have an idea that I was in for a bigger surprise. I had aplenty questions but I decided not to be hasty about them.

"Are you a Sikh?" I asked.

"No, I'm not" he said. I was thrilled. I wanted to know more about the 'mystery guy'.

"Why are you wearing a turban then?" I asked.

"There's a long story behind that but first let me have a look at the poem that you have just written" he said.

I quickly took out the parchment on which I had written the poem and handed it over to him.

He smiled as he read the poem.

"Are you associated with some band?" he asked.

"I'm not yet but yes I will be soon" I said. His eyes lit up.

"And how did you know this?" I said, puzzled.

"Say telepathy, I'm a drummer with a band in Jorhat Engineering College" he answered.

My stomach churned. More surprises were in store for me.

"You are damn creative" he said.

"Every engineer is; thanks for the compliment though" I said.

"But why are you wearing this turban and dressed as a Sikh?" I was still confused. His face turned blue. I could see a pain in his eyes. He refused to answer my question.

"I have sinned" he said. The mystery continued. His answer confused me. I could not comprehend what he said. I thought he was a cryptologist or maybe he didn't want to reveal his secrets. I wanted to know his story badly so. After twenty minutes of persuasion he was finally convinced I was really concerned about the pain that he was going through and he agreed to tell me his story.

Armi meanwhile found nothing interesting in the Sardar and he decided to sleep for a while. He brought with him two cans of beer and he guzzled them down. The Sardar started his heart-breaking story.

A Weedy Tryst

The stage was dimly lit and the quartet played their instruments with such tenacity that the audience came alive after a dull start. Metal Ville had sprung a surprise. They were playing 'Jesus don't want me' by Nirvana. The guitarist stomped his feet on the stage and each chord that they played evoked huge applauses from the audience. The drummer, Mriganka, was the major attraction. He was the best drummer the host college, Jorhat Engineering College had ever produced and he had won the best drummer award twice consecutively with two different bands. Metal-Ville was the third that he had joined.

"It's better to burn out than to fade away" Mriganka or Mig as he was fondly called by his band-mates announced on the microphone. The song ended with a huge battering of the cymbals.

"Acceleration and deceleration" Mig said as he rode his brand new Kawasaki. The speedometer showed 110km/hr and increasing by each passing second.

"You guys are pimps" Nisha shouted into Mig's ears as she tried to prevent a second collision with Mig as he stepped on the brakes. The Kawasaki came to a smooth stop.

"Another close escape" Mig smiled.

"Dare not to touch me" Nisha said, as Mig extended his hands towards the most beautiful pair of assets he had ever seen. He quickly withdrew them.

"How long do I have to wait?" Mig asked.

"Wait till the night we wed" Nisha said, as she ploughed her fingers through Mig's long black hair.

"By that time I'll be a baldy with a walking stick" Mig said, as he skipped and hopped all around Nisha.

Nisha was the girl everyone dreams and would die for. A one man woman, she lived to her promise and now it had been a year since she had entered into a relation with Mig. The third year of Mig's engineering was ending. However, the only thing missing was a union, a physical union rather precisely which had until now become so crucial in every relationship but Mig was never bothered. The only thing about which Mig was bothered was her constant bickering about Mig's addiction to weed. Weed is the American version of what we call cannabis.

"Stop ruining yourself…stop taking drugs" Nisha said, with a look of consternation.

"What about a date tomorrow?" Mig said, trying to evade her dismaying statement.

"You will never listen to me, will you?" Nisha said, her eyes firmly fixed on Mig's deep blue eyes.

"I need to go now; I have an appointment with my other doc" Mig said, as he sped away.

It was weed time. It had grown dark and the appointment with his doc was nothing but an appointment with drugs. He was addicted. As the first puff of smoke gushed into his black lungs, his head spun and twirled. He laughed and cried, all at the same time. He was hallucinating. Nisha flashed through his mind. How beautiful she looked. He had come a long way to have finally loved a woman.

Fourth semester exams had ended and everyone was getting ready for the college's annual fest, Phoenix. Lawns were trimmed and the worn out buildings whitewashed. For Mig, it was one big occasion. He would be performing with his band 'The Tarantula' for the first time.

Backstage, in a dark corner, Mig readied for a fight, a fight against twelve other bands to defend his crown. He took out some powdery stuff and rolled it in a piece of paper ready to light the twelfth cigarette of the day. *Now I'm ready to rock.*

The entire college had assembled. Mig and his drums took the centre stage. The song was 'The man who sold the world' by Nirvana. The guitarist started the rendition playing the perfect riff. The vocalist stretched his vocal chords to the highest pitch possible and Mig hit the cymbals hard, with all his power. The audience loved every bit of the show.

"It's better to burn out than to fade away" Mig pronounced on the microphone amidst huge cheers. He always did so. The song ended but everyone failed to notice Mig. He had collapsed. A white foamy substance oozed out of his mouth. Weed had taken its toll on Mig. He was immediately rushed to a hospital.

"To the ICU" the doc shouted. Mig could faintly hear the commotion all around him. He slowly opened his eyes. He was watching the most beautiful woman he had ever seen.

"Drugs kill" the lady doc said. She had tiny green eyes and Mig felt a sudden twitch in his heart. The doc caressed his hair and Mig fell unconscious. It was a magical touch.

She kept running away from him. The night was growing dark and her body seemed to emanate light illuminating the darkness. Mig ran after her. She wore a white lab coat and short pants and Mig's dark desires grew. Mig ran even faster and held her slender waist from behind. She smiled as Mig kissed on her neck. Mig woke up with a sudden jerk. He had been dreaming all this time.

"Dreaming huh?" the doc asked. Mig was astounded. She was standing right there beside him.

"Was it me?" the doc asked further. *How the fuck did she know that?* Mig went speechless. His face turned red. Mig was a regular at the hospital and they had seen each other before but this was the first time that Dr. Nisha was put in charge of Mig.

"Mr. Mriganka Saikia, 3rd year Mechanical Engineering, JEC, drummer and a drug addict…impressive profile" she said, as she flipped through a stack of white pages of what seemed like Mig's medical report.

"Both drug and doc addict" Mig said, winking at her. The doc laughed aloud.

"Drugs and docs are tantalizingly addictive" the doc said.

"Not all docs but the one whose name I still don't know" Mig said. The doc just couldn't believe her ears. *Some guys actually have brains.*

"Nisha for friends and Dr. Nisha for patients" she seemed equally obtrusive.

"Then I would definitely like call you Nisha" Mig stated in a low, resounding voice. Nisha smiled and nodded.

"I have some appointments, I'll see you later" Nisha said, as she exited the ICU. Mig's cell beeped. A message flashed on the screen.

> *Oh! Baby, heard u collapsed*
> *I was so worried; sorry 4 wat I did and get*
> *well soon.*

Mig quickly deleted the message. He had better things to concentrate on. The sultry Dr. Nisha raced through his mind. This was just the beginning of a fairytale romance.

JEC, once again readied for a season of campus jobs. Salaries were now plummeting with each passing year and before they would hit the rock bottom, Mig decided it was time for him to try and get one.

With Dr. Nisha being at the helm of affairs, Mig recovered within days and the best drummer award for the second time in a row came as a healing touch.

"I hate those HR people...they make you feel like you are sitting inside an interrogation chamber" Mig said. They were sitting at the hospital cafeteria.

"They actually interrogate" Nisha remarked. She was witty and she was fast. The patient-doc relationship was just five days old and the first date was just three hours from materializing. Probably, the first kiss too. Life was fast. Super fast.

"I want to dedicate my entire life to music and rock and wee..." Mig stopped. Nisha had already raised her eyebrows.

"And to weed...stop this bullshit and get yourself a job" Nisha slammed him.

"I'm running after a job at a time when people are running after a blow-job" Mig grinned.

"Stop kidding, a blow-job now may blow your job away" Nisha reiterated. She had to take a stance. After all, it was love at first sight. But Mig, it seemed, was more difficult to understand than she had previously thought.

"I'm leaving; I can't sit here all day inspiring a dumb head" Nisha said, as she picked up her little red bag and walked off.

The preliminary test results were out. Mig was among the sixty students who made it to the second round. These sixty would now battle it out in the second round which was a GD. Mig was fearless and he was almost sure of making the cut.

Sheena sat opposite to Mig and gazed at him constantly. She was wearing a yellow t-shirt with a low neckline, exposing her midriff. Mig's eyes fell on her cleavage. Soon, Mig became so engrossed that he failed to listen to what the HR had said. Mig didn't care. Jobs can come later. It was time to relish the surrounding beauty. Mig was off to his dream world, a world of fantasy where he could seduce any woman he wanted.

"A few words would have been welcomed, Mr. Mriganka" the HR said in a harsh tone. Mig was startled. The HR had probably followed Mig's line of sight.

"Sir, we were talking about malnourishment and its probable effects on future generations" Mig said just at the nick of time. He had sneaked a quick look in his neighbour's notebook. The HR seemed uninterested. Mig had already lost the battle.

"Thank you gentlemen, you can excuse me now" the HR said. Mig walked out. He had screwed up the GD and there was no way he was going in for the interview. Mig called up Nisha.

"Will see you in fifteen minutes; I'm running out of balance" Mig said and hurriedly hung up before Nisha could say a word. The last call duration showed 15 seconds. As soon as he put the phone back into his pocket, his cell beeped. A message flashed on the screen.

Called u umpteen times
No response; I told you I'm sorry?
Msg me urgent

The message disappeared within seconds. He had to reach the hospital.

"I screwed it up; it couldn't have been worse" Mig said.

"What the hell happened?" Nisha asked. She was taken aback.

"Sheena had set up a boob-y trap" Mig said.

"This was the last of the companies" Nisha shrugged after Mig slowly unfolded the events that ended his job hunt. She was acting more like a guardian than a to-be-girlfriend. After all, she was a year older to Mig. Mig's cell beeped. He quickly opened the inbox.

Got thru GD
PI awaits; Congrats

Mig jumped high up in the air and the chair on which he sat fell down with a huge bang. The twenty something people inside the hospital cafeteria looked at him in awe. Mig quickly regained his composure. Nisha was awestruck. She had never seen an exulted Mig. Mig kept gazing at her eyes.

"Why are you looking at me like that?" Nisha said, beaming.

"A recent research suggests that if you look at someone for 8.2 seconds constantly, you will fall in love. I am trying to do exactly that" Mig said. Nisha laughed aloud. The humour Mig possessed floored her. The doctor had fallen for the patient; so had the patient.

"How will you feel if someone takes your hand in the middle of a hospital cafeteria and says those three golden words?" Mig said, doing exactly what he just said. Love was blossoming.

"I'll stab him or push him off a cliff" Nisha said. She knew that Mig was all ready to propose her and she decided not to make it easy for Mig.

"Sad but still I would prefer to get stabbed or pushed off a mountain edge…I love you" Mig muttered the last three words. Nisha didn't have the strength to overpower her emotions.

"Yes" she muttered slowly. Mig leapt up in the air yet again. People turned around but this time he didn't care. He was completely immersed in the doc's love. Nisha sat there smiling away. Mig's dark past was finally erased or Mig thought so.

The interview was much easier than Mig had anticipated. The HR loved his confidence and his cheeky stories.

"You are definitely a spoilt brat but you deserve this job; at least you can entertain me" the HR said at the end of the twenty minute long interview. The day was eventful. Except for the GD, nothing had gone wrong. But looking back, even the GD was much more than enticing. Note down Sheena.

"Let's enact a kissing scene" Mig pestered Nisha. Seven days had passed since Mig had landed a job.

"I do not kiss weedy people" was Nisha's stanch reply. They had shifted their dating location from the hospital cafeteria to the more hip and happening restaurant, Belle Amies.

"But I've stopped taking drugs, now that I've found another more addictive one" Mig said in an obvious reference to Nisha.

"How many ex-girlfriends do you have?" Nisha asked. She knew Mig would lie.

"None" Mig said. He seemed firm and resolute. But every intelligent guy isn't the best liar. That's what Mig forgot. His cell beeped. A message flashed on the screen.

What's on wid u?
Cummon, stop kiddin nd
Take my calls

The message met the same fate as the previous one had. It was quickly deleted.

"Who is it?" Nisha asked. She was curious. The cell beeped repeatedly and Mig cut the line over and over again. Mig was getting doubtful with each passing second.

"Another friend who I think knows about my date today and it seems he's hell bent on disturbing me" Mig said. It wasn't a convincing reply and Nisha smelt a rat. Before Mig could say another word, Nisha swooped down on him and grabbed his phone. Mig could only stare as she began reading messages after messages. Mig could feel Nisha smolder.

"Sir, may I please know who this Jas is?" Nisha asked Mig, tension in the air palpable.

"Ah! I'm sorry; I can explain" Mig stuttered.

"You could have told me about this before" Nisha said.

"Jasmine is my ex" Mig lied again, trying to explain.

"Come back to me once you get over with her" Nisha said. Her eyes had turned red. She was furious. She stood up and walked out of the restaurant. This was something about which Mig had never thought about. He had truly loved Nisha and now she was gone. It felt miserable but Mig couldn't have revealed the truth. He cursed himself. He could have done nothing more.

Every attempt to bring his life back on track was proving to be futile. Slowly but surely, Mig was on the verge of loosing a hard fought battle.

He was broke. He walked out of the restaurant alone. Rain came pouring down and in a deserted corner he took out his medication-cannabis. It was the only thing that never left him alone.

As Mig took his nineteenth puff, his head swirled and he collapsed on the street. *It's better to burn out than to fade away*. People came rushing in and they rushed him to the hospital.

Nisha had just experienced the scariest day of her life. She never imagined in her wildest dreams that Mig would be back at the hospital so soon. Fortunately, those blue eyes opened and Nisha felt relieved.

"You scared the hell out of me, do you even realize that?" Nisha yelled at Mig. Mig smiled.

"You are such a loser" Nisha continued.

"If being a gay or a bisexual is a loser's attribute, yeah, I'm a scum" Mig said. Nisha could not believe her ears. She was dumbfounded.

"What do you mean?" Nisha mumbled. Her throat dried up.

"I don't know who I'm; all my life I've been labeled as an outcast just because of my sexual inclination" Mig said. An eerie silence crept in the cabin. Nisha listened.

"If you think I'm a gay, you might be wrong because of the fact that I love you and if you think I am straight, you are wrong because of the fact that I loved a man. Jas is Shrejas" Mig continued with his stunning revelations.

"Who the hell am I? I have no idea. Why did I fall in love with a man and then a woman? I have no idea. I have no answers" Mig disclosed further. Nisha's eyes swelled up and a drop of tear rolled down her cheek as secrets came tumbling out of the closet.

"Why do you think I smoke weed? Because it helps me forget that

I'm an outcast, a recluse" Mig said. Nisha burst into tears and ran out of the room. Her mind stopped working. She loved Mig but she could not live with a man with bisexual tendencies.

"I'm sorry Mig, I can't live with you" Nisha said. Tears were still flowing. Mig nodded.

As Mig narrated to me the gripping tale of his survival, I could only express my heartfelt sympathies for the man who had struggled against all odds and was still fighting for his life. I had too many questions to ask but I decided to wait until the story was completed.

"But why are you disguised as a Sardar?" I said.

"Actually I had to put on a disguise" Mig said.

"I don't understand" I said.

"There is a story behind that too" Mig replied. I braced myself for another adventure.

Just another summer night

Mig was certainly different from others. He never studied but still scored the best grades. He had little or no friends and always lived alone. Very few people knew about the 'mystery guy'. Rumours were flying thick and fast. Some said that Mig was the son of a dreaded ULFA leader; other said that he was a drug peddler. Some tagged him as a loner while some admitted seeing him perform black magic and voodoos.

A square rugged face and plenty of scars, leftovers of numerous crushed pimples, a height which was the envy of many a guys, long dark hair and deep blue eyes- an image of a rock star. Mig's rugged features had a stark resemblance to Cobain. His only friends were Cannabis and Facebook. He was hooked to both. He was a child prodigy and started playing on the drums from the age of six but his reserved nature proved to be a hurdle on the way of demonstrating his talent to the world. He started following Cobain and his life from the very onset and loved the way Nirvana performed. Mig was deeply influenced by his antics.

Now he had an opportunity to showcase his talent to the world. The passion was visible. He wanted to be a rock star and Denigrado was the first step towards that direction. Denigrado was the only band which played original grunge compositions. They called themselves 'grungy metal freaks'. When the drummer passed out of the college, Mig was quickly absorbed and he became the new face of the band. Within six months of Mig's arrival, Denigrado won two inter-college rock fests and qualified for a few state level competitions. They were dominating the local rock circuit.

Rishabh, Jeremy and Gaurav were his band mates and Mig's first friends in college. But everything changed one day when he revealed a dark hidden truth.

"Get another drink for me" Mig said. Rishabh had already burned out. Only Jeremy and Gaurav sat beside him strumming their guitars.

"Call that bitch" Jeremy laughed back.

"Mig loves that bitch, isn't it?" Gaurav teased Mig.

"I just love certain things about Sheena and you know about those" Mig said.

"I know that she will even wipe your ass if you ask her to" Jeremy said. The two laughed aloud. Everyone knew about Sheena's crush on Mig.

"Why don't you ask her out?" Gaurav popped a quick question.

"No offence but I do not have a crush on her, here goes my weed" Mig said clearing the air yet again.

"Good man! I heard that she's a lesbian and she likes boys with girly features" Jeremy said, taking a dig at Mig.

"What is the problem if one is a lesbian, a gay or a bisexual? What's the big deal about it? Everyone has a life; live and let live, after all they too are humans" Mig slammed the two. Weed was slowly showing its effects.

"Gays are nothing but cheap trash. They are a disgrace to our societal ethics and morals" Jeremy shouted on top of his voice. Mig was unfazed. He was used to this moral preaching stuff.

"You hate gays? Well sorry, I don't and being a friend let me tell you something today- I am a gay and I don't hide things and I'm walking out of your band" Mig said as he walked out of the room. Jeremy and Gaurav were shell shocked. They couldn't believe what they had just heard. Outside, Mig lighted up a cigarette. It was pouring and he made his way towards his room. *A gay equals to a scum*. The stigma attached with being a gay was getting unbearable now.

Mig turned on his computer and lighted up his cigarette. The GPRS connection was slow and opening Facebook was one of the toughest ordeals he had ever faced. But then, he met Shrejas through Facebook. When everyone hated him, Shrejas was the only one who lent a shoulder to him.

The page finally opened. He opened the inbox which showed seven new messages, all from Shrejas. He deleted each one of them. His mind drifted to a year ago when he had first met the guy who made him realize about the dark truths.

"He looks like a gay; stay away from him" Mig heard his classmate whisper. Schooling couldn't have been worse.

"Taunt me assholes but I'm gonna show each one of you who and what I am" Mig yelled at his classmate. Mig did have some amount of feminine features and this attracted more insult. He was even jeered at by his teachers.

"Marry a guy and he will protect you" his classmate mocked him. Mig tried to be strong but when the entire class erupted in laughter, he could do nothing but run away. That day, Mig resolved that he would become a man.

He started injecting and inhaling cocaine. No drug was spared. Mig joined gyms and built up his body. Within six months, he had changed so much so that even girls began to love him. And none other than Shrejas helped him in that tumultuous period. The chance meeting proved to be the biggest surprise life had ever thrown at him.

"Are you Mriganka Barua?" a message popped inside the inbox.

"You have got the surname wrong" Mig replied back.

"Mriganka what then?" another message popped inside.

"Mriganka Saikia; what's your name?" Mriganka wrote back.

"Oh! I'm sorry; by the way I'm Shrejas Bhullar; 1st year engineering" he replied. Mig quickly checked out his profile. It seemed impressive. The display picture showed a handsome young man. For the first time in his life, he felt a twitch in his heart. It was bizarre.

"Never mind, now that you have found Mriganka, we can be friends, can't we?" Mig wrote. Mig had no real friends and he loved making virtual friends.

"Of course we can" Shrejas replied. This was the beginning of a very intimate friendship.

Within months, Mig came to know about the similarities their life shared. Shrejas had not many friends to hang out with as did Mig and they both were drug addicts. The two friends bared their hearts out to each other. Mig developed a deep sense of sympathy for Shrejas or this was what he thought so. Mig had no idea whatsoever that he was slowly falling in love with a man. Shrejas, on the other hand, had already fallen for Mig. But the fear of losing a friend troubled him and he hesitated to make his feelings clear.

Not being able to keep his feelings hidden inside his heart any longer, Shrejas decided it was time to open his heart. On a fine Sunday night, he finally did.

"Hey, what's going on?" Shrejas wrote.

"Just came back from my tuitions and getting ready for dinner" Mig said.

"I wanted to tell you something today" Shrejas wrote.

"Yeah sure, please" Mig replied, unknown to what was about to come.

"I think I'm in love with you" Shrejas held his breath as he said. Mig dropped his jaw. His mind stopped working. He had no idea what he would do.

"You can take as much time as you want" Shrejas continued.

"I'll think about it and I have to go now" Mig said. Mig had to take the toughest decision of his life. If he rejected he would loose a friend, the best friend. If he accepted, the society would ostracize him.

"I see you tomorrow" Shrejas said as he went offline.

The night was long. Terrible dreams haunted him all night. He wanted to kill himself every time he thought about his fucked up life. He had no friends and he couldn't loose another one. Finally after much deliberation, he found the answer. He waited for Monday night and it didn't take much time.

"Hey Mig, how was you day" a message popped into his inbox as soon as he went online.

"It was fantastic; another girl tried to molest me today" Mig replied.

"Lol, what did you do?"

"I let her do what she wanted to"

"Lol, and what did she do?" Shrejas was laughing. He liked the humour and Mig's sexually explicit adventures.

"It was actually a series of events" Mig wrote.

"I want to know" Shrejas said.

"In the tuition class, she sat beside me and kept staring at me. When

I looked at her, she touched my thigh and slowly her hands made their way to the Virgin Islands. Of course I was enjoying every moment and I didn't obstruct her. But looking at her after a few minutes, I could say that she was freaked out because the island's volcano remained dormant" Mig explained.

"Lolzzz….I can't believe this. You will make me cry" Shrejas just couldn't stop laughing. Tears were rolling down and he felt he would get a heart attack. He loved Mig's dark humour more than anything else. The laugh riot was finally over.

"Thought about what I said?" Shrejas asked.

"I didn't think much about what you said, I just thought about Shrejas" Mig replied.

"What did you think about Shrejas?" Shrejas said. Fear lurked inside him but he managed to put up a brave face.

"A very down to earth, honorable, adorable, a great friend and a person with whom I have no hesitation to live with" Mig said. He could hear Shrejas scream in exultation.

"When do I come to meet you?" Shrejas said.

"Whenever you feel like" Mig wrote back. Mig still had doubts. But when he visualized Shrejas he felt better. He was in love too. Everything went on smoothly till Mig passed out of school and got an admission in JEC.

⸙

It was almost six months since Mig had first met Shrejas and they couldn't have been happier. A huge surprise was in store for Mig.

One bright Sunday morning, Mig's cell beeped. Mig quickly picked up the call.

"Hey Mig, can you spare some time tomorrow?" It was Shrejas. Mig was taken aback at his sudden question.

"Yeah, I can" Mig said.

"Then be there at Guwahati tomorrow, I have a flight from Delhi" Shrejas said. It was a bolt from the blue. He had a hard time believing the fact that Shrejas would be undertaking a 2500 km journey just for him.

"Wow! I can't believe this. Love ya" Mig couldn't stop himself.

"Love ya darling; I'll see you tomorrow" Shrejas said as he hung up. Adrenaline flowed through Mig's body as he thought about the surprises that would be in store for him. Mig just couldn't wait for his arrival.

The day was bright and sunny and Mig arrived early at the airport but he didn't have to wait long. The flight arrived fifteen minutes earlier than the scheduled time. As Mig watched the passengers come out of the terminal one by one, a young handsome lad waved at him. His hair was brushed backwards and he wore a grey suit which was complemented by a thin frameless glass and a light blue necktie. Mig smiled and waved back at him. The charismatic Shrejas floored him almost instantly.

"How was your journey?" Mig said, as he shook hands with Shrejas.

"Absolutely fantastic but I missed you" Shrejas smiled.

"I missed you too" Mig said. Emotions overwhelmed him.

"Let's not be too much sentimental; I have come here not to cry but to spend time with you and talk about the tough life ahead" Shrejas said. Mig nodded. Deep inside Mig knew that it would be difficult for them to live life together forever. He had prepared himself for the worst.

"I'm hungry, get me a bite" Shrejas said. The couple headed to a nearby restaurant.

"I've got something for you" Shrejas said, his eyes sparkling.

"I hate gifts" Mig said. Shrejas smiled and Mig watched in awe as he took out two tickets.

"Two tickets to Darjeeling" Shrejas said. Mig nodded.

"We leave in an hour" Shrejas said.

The charisma and the flamboyance of the man sitting beside him stirred Mig's soul. Shrejas had to be his soul mate. Now it didn't matter whether Shrejas was a man or a woman. He had found someone who loved him and understood him the way no one ever did. All doubts lurking inside his mind were washed away.

The beautiful snow capped mountains of the Himalayas beckoned. Shrejas had a special reason to visit Darjeeling with Mig and this would probably be the last time he would be seeing Mig.

"Wow! This is beautiful, this is the most beautiful sight I've ever seen" Shrejas exclaimed as he stepped out of the cab. The giant mountains welcomed him.

"This is Darjeeling for you" Mig said.

"A hot cup of Darjeeling tea would have worked wonders to my freezing body" Shrejas remarked. The temperature dropped below freezing point and even the heavy woolens were failing to keep them warm. Mig ordered a cup of hot tea and the couple sat on a bench watching the sun set in the distant horizon behind the mountains.

"I've got something to tell you" Shrejas said as he clutched Mig's hands tightly.

"Go ahead"

"Look at those mountains, they stand strong and no force on earth can shake them. Do you know what holds them?" Shrejas explained, the philosopher in him coming alive.

"The strength and the will power to remain standing no matter how much the winds and the quakes try to uproot them, you will have to be the same. You will have to fight every obstacle that comes your way" Shrejas explained as tears came flowing out.

"But why are you saying me all these?" Mig said. He was astonished at Shrejas' sudden outburst.

"I'm sorry; it was a sudden surge of emotions" Shrejas said. They both hugged each other. The icy cold winds forced the two to return back to the hotel for the night.

"Hot chicken dumplings, chicken corn soup and lots of salad, what can be more delicious?" Shrejas said. Shrejas loved chicken but this was the first time he was trying Tibetan cuisine and he loved every bite.

"Aww! I almost choked" Shrejas remarked. He tried to swallow a mammoth chicken dumpling which almost got stuck inside his throat and Mig had to force it inside his tummy.

"Thank you so much Mig for being a part of my life" Shrejas clutched his hands tightly. A sudden surge of emotions overwhelmed Mig and for the first time they kissed each other. Mig quickly withdrew himself. His heart beat faster as he tried to see into Shrejas' eyes. There was something about those eyes which sucked Mig into them every time he gazed at them. The rest of the night they spent holding each other in their arms and making love. At the crack of dawn, the couple readied to leave after their most romantic trip ever.

"Goodbye Mig" Shrejas wished as he entered the boarding terminal. This was his most memorable experience.

"Goodbye Shrejas" Mig wished him in return. Mig enjoyed every bit of the journey with Shrejas.

Shrejas never called Mig again. He deleted his Facebook account, changed all his phone numbers and never replied to Mig's mails. Mig felt cheated. After innumerable attempts to contact him failed, Mig suffered a massive depression. In college, he wouldn't talk to anyone. He stopped playing drums and cannabis became his life.

Three months into the start of the second year of Mig's engineering, Nisha entered his life and changed it completely. A year later Mig suddenly started receiving messages and calls from Shrejas and that's when Nisha realized the truth about Mig and she left him.

I sat still as Mig's story unfolded. For the first time it became clear to me that life is in fact like a roller-coaster-one moment you are on a high and the next moment you can face the worst moment life can ever throw at you. I had plenty of questions in my mind but I decided not to be hasty about them.

"But the question remains. Why are you disguised as a Sardar?" I asked.

"According to Shrejas' family traditions, they don't allow non-Sikhs to attend a family funeral" Mig answered. My jaw dropped. My neurons ceased to work and I felt I would suffer a sudden bout of paralysis.

"Yeah, you are right…Shrejas died of cancer last week. I got the news from one of his friends in Facebook and I wanted to see him for one last time. That's how I'm here with you" Mig said. Apparently, Shrejas had tried to tell Mig about the last few days that he would spend on this earth and cancer was the only reason why he had stopped talking to Mig.

"Where's Nisha now?" I asked.

"She's still in Jorhat"

"Did you try and talk to her after she left?" I was curious to know more. Mig was a true lover and I wanted him to stay happy.

"She hates me for what I'm" Mig said.

"I can give you an idea which might just work." I said. My plans seldom worked but ideas surely became a hit. Mig was excited. He loved Nisha and he wanted to woo her back.

"The next time you perform on stage, sing Enrique's Hero, it has been lucky for me" I said, as I remembered singing this song for Shreya which if not anything, changed her tastes. Jokes apart, this song blew her mind away and I felt, this song had the power to sweep any woman off their feet.

"Sure, I'll give it a shot" Mig smiled.

"We are starting a band; I, Armaan, Jerry and we needed a drummer. Would you like to be part of our band?" I just couldn't stop myself. I knew Mig wouldn't reject my proposal. I strongly believed in destiny and destiny was taking me to where I belonged. Mig thought hard. I checked out my watch. It was 4:30 in the morning and Armi was snoring.

"I'll think about it" Mig replied. The train finally arrived at the New Delhi railway station and I wished Mig all the luck. We waved goodbye and promised to call each other every now and then. Sleep was slowly creeping into my eyes and Agra was still three hours away. I decided to sleep.

I wasn't in my deepest sleep and as the train came to a screeching halt something hit my butt.

"Wake up metal-head" he shouted and kicked me for the second time.

"You are such a pain in the ass" I remarked.

"Get up now or else you will get washed off along with this train" he said.

I looked at my watch. It showed 6:30. We had finally reached Agra. On the way to the hostel, I told everything about the mysterious Sardar. He, at first thought I was making it up bust as I continued, he was perplexed beyond imagination. I was amused by his facial expressions which changed every time the story had a new twist.

Reaching the hostel, I took a bath and dozed off.

The Hippocratic Oath

Mig was a bisexual and initially I had reservations but he was one of the finest human beings I had ever met and going by his records and the number of awards that he had won, I could surely say that I had found a gem. And his sexual inclination had nothing to do with his extraordinary talent. I absolutely admired and adored him.

Armi's tryst with the guitar continued and he became a little more eccentric because the number of girls he entertained now almost doubled. He fantasized about almost all the girls including those '*behenjis*' and every night his erotic screams would echo inside my ears. I would ask him to scream louder and he would do it with pride. The nights were horrific. So were the days. This continued for a month until he thought he had found his perfect love. And so it seemed.

"Hey thinass, I want to show you something" Mig came running towards me. He tried to pull me but I resisted. Every time, the weirdo wanted to show me something, it would either be a lacy bra clearly visible through a white transparent shirt or a pair of popping nipples. I had seen thousands.

"What is it weirdo?"

"Come naa" Armi said. He wouldn't relent.

The library looked relatively different, different because I was visiting it after a gap of one and a half years. A girl sat on the farthest corner studying an encyclopedia.

"How is she?" Armi said, pointing towards her. Armi's eccentricity had crossed limits. I agree she was beautiful, but she was just half the size of Armi. And the most surprising of all was the fact that she was reading an encyclopedia. We liked reading Cosmopolitans and Penthouses.

"If I go by what she's reading, she's definitely not someone you would like to get hooked to" I said.

"I might just be able to clear your doubts" Armi winked at me. He pulled me towards her. Seeing us, the girl hurriedly closed the giant book. I wondered what she was up to.

"Hey, sweet honey, meet Samarth" Armi said, introducing me to her. I nodded in approval.

"And Samarth, meet Olive, my favourite fresher" Armi said. She smiled. True to her name, she was an envoy of peace-clumsy and lethargic. The only saving grace was her sex-appeal, those beautifully sculptured legs which almost took me to fantasy land.

"I was reading this encyclopedia, actually I like exploring things" she said smiling at me. I smiled back. Armi had certainly found something useful after his guitar.

"Oh! Absolutely fantastic; keep it up" I complimented her.

"Olive, show her what you were actually exploring" Ami said. I saw that devilish expression on his face which would come out every time he would hunt someone down. Olive's face turned red. She was embarrassed and she felt humiliated but nothing could stop Armi now.

"Baby, you know how much I love you and Samarth doesn't mind anything" Armi said. It was emotional blackmailing on the sweet girl but Armi was hell bent in proving me that his choice would never be wrong. Slowly, she opened the encyclopedia. Hidden neatly inside was a copy of the Kamasutra. She was embarrassed and insulted. I chided Armi. Armi couldn't stop laughing.

"I'm sorry Olive; I was just joking" Armi said. All this while, Olive hadn't said a word. But now it was her turn.

"Sorry my foot; go to hell Armaan Sharma" she screamed. Armi went after her but Armi had gone too far. The insult was grave and Armi learnt his lesson when she promised she would never talk to him ever again. Fifth semester rolled by.

On the fourteenth day of the second month of the fifth semester, Mig called me up. I became pretty sure that our search for a drummer was finally over.

"How's everything going?" Mig asked.

"Horrendous, the thermometer will surely burst in the coming few days" I said. My room temperature was 43 degrees.

"Nisha's back with me; your plan worked" he said gleefully.

"Congrats mate, that's the best news I've had in a while" I said. I wanted to see the man happy and my plan helped him to gain that happiness, I was glad that he had finally found his love.

"Thanks for everything" Mig said.

"Not to mention but tell me how you wooed her; tell me everything from scratch" I said. I had anticipated yet another incredible adrenaline pumping tale and it turned out to be exactly that.

It was a year since Mig and Nisha hadn't talked to each other. Farewell was approaching fast and this was the only opportunity to woo Nisha back. But before that he wanted to check out certain things. He drew up a plan.

He smoked cigarettes after cigarettes all stuffed with substantial amount of cannabis until he collapsed. Of course, he did it deliberately and kept a junior beside him. The junior was entrusted with the job of admitting him to the hospital. And he did.

Nisha was sitting at the hospital cafeteria with her colleagues when news of her former patient boyfriend being hospitalized reached her.

"What? This guy will always remain a pimp" Nisha mumbled as she made her way to cabin no-33 where Mig was admitted.

"Will you ever stop stuffing yourself with drugs?" she clamoured at him.

"I was addicted to some other drug but that drug hates me; so this is the only option" Mig shrugged. Mig thought he would lighten up the mood but Nisha gave him a stern look.

"It's pathetic, the way you land at the hospital every second Sunday and flirt with me" Nisha said.

"Flirting means to lie; I'm telling you the truth" Mig said.

"Mind your own business, dude" Nisha said, as she turned around and walked away.

"At least check whether I'm all right" Mig's pleas fell into deaf ears.

Three hours later, Mig suddenly woke up. All this time he had been sleeping. He felt someone caressing his hair. He at once recognized the touch. Mig slowly opened one of his eyes. It was Nisha. The care was evidence to the fact that she still had feelings for him. He desperately wanted to kiss her and hold her in her arms but he restrained himself. The first part of his plan was over. Now he had to work on the second part, the toughest part, Sheena.

The plan was to take Sheena to a date at the hospital cafeteria with Nisha in sight. Now that he knew that Nisha still loved him, it would be great to watch her get envious. But it wasn't easy to convince Sheena for a date.

"Hi! How's everything going?" Mig said. Sheena was stunned. This was probably the first time that Mig had such sweet words for her. She smelt a rat.

"Are you perfectly all right Mr. Mriganka?" she asked. It was a pretty unusual start to a rather dull Friday morning.

"I am perfectly all right" Mig said. Sheena was sitting on the stairway leading to the Engineering Drawing labs and Mig stood in front her. His eyes fell on her finely polished twin assets and the GD flashed back to his mind. He always relished watching those.

"Sit down Mig, is there anything I can help you with?" she asked. Mig sat down. It was difficult sitting with Sheena. Every now and then, his eyes would fall on her enticers and Sheena would slap on his wrist.

"Would you like to go on a date with me?" Mig finally said after seven attempts. Sheena erupted in joy as she heard this. Apparently, she thought that Mig was going to propose her on the date and she readily agreed.

Sunday arrived and it was time for Mig to execute the second part of the plan. Sheena was the happiest. This was the day she had always dreamed about. She wore olive green camouflaged short pants which showed off her long and beautiful legs and a top which showed five centimeters of her cleavage and ended just above the navel. For the first time, Mig saw her finely toned body and rued the fact that he was in love with someone who wouldn't even allow herself to be touched.

"Where are we going?" Nisha asked. Nisha expected that Mig would take her to some swanky restaurant and that's when she received the first shock.

"To the hospital cafeteria" Mig answered.

"What? Are you crazy, a date in the hospital cafeteria?" She almost yelled out. Mig had a pretty good explanation in store for her.

"Actually, I am not really feeling well today; I smoked seven cocaine stuffed cigarettes the night before and I might just collapse, so I thought of spending time together in the cafeteria" Mig said. Sheena finally relented after cross examining Mig and making sure that he had indeed smoked seven cocaine stuffed cigarettes.

Nisha was sitting all alone in one of the farthest corners of the café and she was stunned to see Mig along with Nisha as they took their table. Mig was hard to understand, harder than anyone. She continued sipping her coffee without showing a reaction.

On the other side, Mig waited for a reaction. There wasn't any. He took Sheena's hands into his own and began stroking them. Sheena smiled but Mig's eyes were somewhere else. From the corner of his eyes, he could see Nisha. She got up and walked out of the café.

"Yeahhh…!" Mig leapt up in the air as Nisha vanished from the view. Nisha still loved him and the time had come to woo her back. He felt a tug on his shirt. It was Sheena. She was shocked at his eccentric behaviour.

"You didn't propose me and I didn't accept your proposal yet" she said. Mig could not stop laughing and ran out of the café without saying a word.

"Son of a bitch" Mig heard Sheena yell from behind but he didn't care. What he cared now for was his master plan.

The farewell day arrived. Mig had to perform along with his band Metal-Ville. Mig had drawn up huge plans. The crowd assembled and Metal-Ville readied for their final performance.

Metal-Ville was a metal band and everyone expected them to play a Pantera or a Slayer or a Sepultura but what they played took everyone by surprise. It was Enrique Iglesius's 'Hero' and the lead singer's position was taken by the best drummer Mig.

"You might be surprised but tonight I'm performing for a lady" Mig announced on the microphone. The audience welcomed him with a loud cheer.

"Here goes Hero by Enrique" Mig announced as he started the rendition. The crowd cheered and clapped every note the Metal-Ville played. The song ended and Mig invited Nisha on stage. But she was nowhere to be seen.

"I request Dr. Nisha to come on stage" Mig announced the second time. But there was no response. Mig stepped out of the stage dejected. May be, Nisha never loved him. Backstage, he sat alone on a stairway. The guilt was killing him. Suddenly, he felt a tug from behind. He turned around only to fine Nisha standing right there in front of his very eyes.

"What happened to Sheena?" Nisha said.

"That was just a gimmick; she says that I'm the son of a bitch" Mig replied.

"I knew what you were up to"

"Then what are we waiting for?" Mig smiled. Nisha jumped into his arms and people clapped and cheered as Mig held her tightly in his arms. His plan worked and so did my idea. Nisha was back in his life.

"Take an oath" Nisha said.

"What oath?" Mig was confused.

"Take an oath that you will never leave me alone" Nisha said.

"I never will honey" Mig said. After a thousand more pledges and oaths that Mig would never touch drugs, Nisha kissed Mig for the first time. The story didn't end here. For the first time since Mig and Nisha became a couple, Nisha let Mig touch her. Mig showed his expertise in handling things and all his fantasies came true.

"Man! I didn't know you could be so romantic" I said as Mig's story unfolded.

"Thanks buddy, it wouldn't have been possible without your support" Mig said.

"It's perfectly fine" I said,

"And there's another news, my company has posted me at Delhi; I'll think about the band once I reach there" Mig said. I was exulted. It couldn't have been better. I knew that my dream of forming a band was slowly but surely coming true.

"That's great; I'll see you soon" I said. Mig hung up.

The Metallic Lady

APL or Agra Premier League was nearing by the day. If you haven't heard about this league, I take this opportunity to tell you that APL is a FIFA gaming competition between four guys, all vying for the coveted prize of a Pepsi My Can, a packet of Benson and hedges and the crown- The APL champion. But the last two times I won it, I didn't get an ounce of what I had to. With Armi out of practice for quite a while now, I found myself at an advantageous position. Among the four of us only Armi gave a good fight.

The other two –Ankit and Bodu (pronounced as b-o-r-u) were nerds and were still learning the nuances of the game. In case you haven't understood what the name BODU means, there is a sweet small story that changed Bhagwan Bodu's life forever.

Once, Bodu went on a sightseeing trip to Jaipur along with a set of friends. Our Bodu was a card addict and no one could beat him in that game. They decided to play a game of cards. Bodu was the undisputed champion but that day, something more was in store for him.

Bodu lost each and every game that he played. Soon he was in a trauma like condition. Mental depression had settled in him. On the way the bus stopped at a 'dhaba' where they got off. Bodu decided to spend some time alone. He stood near the bus thinking about the mistakes that he made while playing and which cost him his undisputed championship title.

Meanwhile his friends were gobbling up the snacks that they were offered. At a distance one of them saw Bodu limping around as he came towards them.

"Hey, what happened? Why are you limping?" asked one of his friends.

"Man, I'm retiring from this card game" Bodu answered.

"Why? What happened?" asked another one.

"Actually, I was standing beside the bus when someone puked and the entire thing just dropped on my head. I went to the toilet to wash myself. On the way, lights went off and in the ensuing darkness, I failed to notice a ditch filled with water. I fell straight into it. I got up; water had soaked me and my shoes. I took my shoes off and proceeded towards the bathroom to wash myself only to slip again. "Oops! My shoulder hurts" he said, finally making an end to a long story.

There was a silence for sometime and then everyone burst out laughing.

"Oh! You are such a baudam my dear" one of his friends remarked.

That day onwards, he came to be known as Baudam and within three weeks its shorter version Bodu arrived. Soon after that, Bodu left playing cards and took to playing FIFA hoping to leave a mark but till today he has been largely unsuccessful.

D-day arrived. Armi bought specially designed bandages for his bleeding fingers. The other two arrived fully armed with joysticks and gamepads. Computers were connected and the extravaganza started.

The first game was played between the underdogs, Ankit and Bodu. Bodu won the match 2-0. The next match was the most awaited one. It was between Armi and me. Armi opened his account in the sixth minute scoring from a corner. In the twenty-first minute, I scored from a stunning free kick. None of us could break the deadlock until the sixty-fourth minute when I increased my lead to 2-1. My worst fears came true when Armi equalized in the eighty-ninth minute. There was still a minute left when Armi scored again and took the game away from me.

The next two encounters were one sided ones with Armi beating Bodu 4-0 and I beating Ankit 5-1. In the next match, however, I managed to save my skin and managed to salvage a draw with Bodu who held his breath till the ninetieth minute. However, Armi beat Ankit again and sat pretty on top of the table.

The next match between me and Armi was a nail biting affair. The game lasted a full ninetieth minute without anyone scoring. There was still thirty minutes of extra time. In the hundred and fifteenth minute, I scored from a penalty. I knew I had won until the goalkeeper stopped it and I had missed my best chance. Finally, in the hundred and seventeenth minute, I scored a stunner from thirty yards and won the match.

Armi walked out of the room dejected. A few minutes later, I heard a smashing sound come out of his room. I thought he had smashed his skull. I rushed out. Entering his room, I found him standing beside his guitar, which was smashed beyond recognition.

"What have you done?" I said, screaming at him.

"I have just smashed my curse" he said.

"Don't the fuck you know that it costs a fucking four thousand bucks?" I said, slowly increasing the frequency of the F-word.

"I'm never gonna play this instrument again" he roared.

"Just because, you lost something which was nothing more than a mere pastime, that doesn't mean that you stop playing the guitar or smash it" I said, trying to make the egotist in him to understand.

"I do not want to hear anything right now. Please get out of my room" he ordered.

For the next five days, we didn't talk. It was painful but I wanted to know how egotists thought like. More precisely, I became a fucked up egotist.

Classes were on in full swing along with proxies and '*netagiri*'. There were three classes of students in our college.

1. The nerds who had no idea what they were here for.

2. The geeks who would stick to the study table even if a volcano erupted a kilometer away and

3. The *netas,* who were busy solving problems that arose between the other two classes, but the fact, was that they were happy aggravating those problems rather than solving them.

I belonged to the first class- the nerds, busy in their creative pursuits rather than their course study. I hated the third classes- the *netas.*

Armi still wasn't talking to me. In the classes we sat on the different benches, and for the first time made notes on a different notebook. The sound of guitar ceased to come out of Armi's room.

The formation of our band was still playing on my mind. I had found all my members and I just wanted to bring them together. I decided to call Jerry.

"Hi, Jerry, how are you?" I asked.

"Hi, Samarth, I'm fine here" he said.

"Actually, I wanted to talk to you about the band" he said

"Yeah, Sure why don't you come to Delhi, we can plan it" he said.

"When are you free?" I asked

"Sunday, I'll be at home if you can come" he said

"Ok! I'll be there on Sunday" I said.

"See you then, bye" he said.

"Bye, Jerry" I said and cut the line.

Saturday night was peaceful until I heard a knock on door.

"Who is it?" I said and cut the line.

There was no reply. The knocking continued. I opened the door. There were three guys whom I recognized as my seniors. They barged into my room and I could do nothing to stop them. They were heavily drunk and I was terrified. I wished Armi was here. One of them sat beside my computer and began an intensive search. I was surprised because I was neither a Pakistani spy nor were they RAW agents. With a prodigious '*tika*' on each of the faces, I realized that the third class had arrived.

The other two meanwhile started an interrogation session.

"*Bahut laundiyabaji karta hai*" one of them said.

"No, no… Sir, there's nothing like that" I stammered.

I wanted to run away. I knew that the guys wouldn't let me spend the night in peace. I doubted if I would survive the night. One of them picked up a baseball bat. Unfortunately, that bat came to my room the day before when one of my classmates had thrashed his junior with it and he wanted to hide it somewhere. More unluckily, I gave him the permission to hide it in my room.

"Stop talking to that girl or else face the consequences" the three of them roared in unison.

I felt a lump in my throat. One blow of a baseball bat can send you packing to the hospital.

And then like a hero from some bollywood masala flick, he arrived. Yes, it was none other than Armi. With one blow, he knocked down the one sitting beside the computer. The one with the baseball bat swung it towards Armi, but before that Armi's kick had reached the periphery of his tummy. He fell down groaning in pain. The third one had already disappeared and soon the other two were also gone.

I looked at Armi. He still wouldn't talk to me. *What a fucking egotist?*

I thought. I tried to start a conversation.

"I'm really sorry about that day" I said.

"Oh! Come on! You are making me sentimental" he said, smiling.

We both hugged each other and the Samarth-Armi combination resumed its journey. Soon, alcohol made its way and we both drank till our guts churned and turned.

The next day, we sat together to discuss our plans. I told him about Mig and Jerry and that they had agreed to start a band and Armi volunteered to go with me. In the evening, I was sitting and completing the few assignments when I heard the sound of the six-string coming out of Armi's room. I was exhilarated.

I rushed into his room to find him playing him on his brand new guitar.

"Where did you get this?" I asked.

"I didn't get this, I bought this" he answered.

"Oh! You are so good" I said and cuddled him.

"Stop doing this and listen to this new chord which I learnt today" he said.

"Oh! No! Not again" I said and returned to my room.

The week passed off without anymore glitches. Armi did a rendition of the beautiful Enrique song '*Hero*' and that reminded me of the day I had proposed Shreya. I was eagerly waiting for Sunday.

The sky was bright and clear on Sunday morning and we took the Intercity Express to Delhi. The guitar had already taken my place in Armi's life and now he carried it with him anywhere and everywhere he went. That day was the same.

Talking about girls, I thought Armi was one of the greatest flirts of all time. He loved flirting but love was never his cup of tea. Himesh Reshamiya had now taken a back seat. He would drink and blab about being like Kurt Cobain and that he would someday visit Aberdeen to lay a wreath on his grave. I, on the other hand would stick to his music.

In the train, a pretty twenty-something girl sat on the opposite seat. She was chatting away on her phone. The train wasn't much crowded and we could hear her conversation.

"Go to hell, I never want to talk to you again" she said. Apparently, she was talking to her boyfriend. There was a silence and then she erupted again.

"It's fine, I don't even care. There was silence again.

"Bye" she cut the line.

There was a long silence. Armi kept looking at me without saying a single word. It was strange but I realized that something was going on in Armi's mind. Finally, after seven long minutes he spoke.

"Seems like she had a breakup" he said.

"How can I know? May be she had" I said.

"But why are you asking this?" I asked further.

"Because she's pretty" he said as I saw him unzipping his guitar cover.

"Hey, which song did you sing when you proposed Shreya?" Armi asked.

"Hero" I answered.

"Here it goes..." Armi said.

Armi began his rendition and I sang along with him. The combination seemed perfect. Armi was flawless on his guitar. As the song ended, the girl began clapping. A small crowd had also gathered and they clapped their hands along with the notes and I understood that English music had penetrated into inner India. Armi and I stood up and bowed up before the crowd and the gesture was reciprocated with a thunderous applause. Before I had blinked my eye, Armi had already started flirting.

"Hi, I'm Armaan. May I know your name?" he asked.

"Ayushi" she replied in a heavily accented tone.

"Nice name, huh" Armi said.

"Thanks, can you play another one?" she said.

"Sure, which song would you like to hear?" Armi asked.

"Anything very romantic" she answered.

"Okay, we'll sing for you James Blunt" Armi said.

"Thank you, I just love him" she said.

We started singing.

You are beautiful, it's true
I saw you face, in a crowded place
And I don't know what to do

The song struck a chord with Ayushi and she was instantly floored.

"Wow! That was great" she remarked.

"Thank you" we said.

"Can you lend me your guitar?" she said after a brief pause.

I wondered what she would do with it. *What if she knows to play the instrument*? Armi handed the guitar to her.

"Actually I'm a huge fan of Metallica and thrash metal" she said, as she started playing on it a tune which I recognized was *Unforgiven-2* by Metallica. I was shocked. I moved my eyeballs slowly towards Armi. He was sitting still, almost senseless. An egotist he was, I knew he could not digest the fact that a girl was giving him tough competition. I could see his ears glowing red. Her rendition was as perfect as Kirk

Hammett himself.

"That was even more beautiful" I said, appreciating what she had just played. Armi was fuming. I wondered if she was an American.

"Thank you" she said.

"What do you do?" I asked Ayushi.

"I'm a western music undergraduate student at Cambridge" she answered. This was more shocking. She handed over the guitar to Armi. I could feel temperatures rising. Armi was burning.

"Why a vocalist does always takes the honours?" he asked.

"Why don't you ask for her number?" I whispered into his ears.

"Ayushi, can we have your number please? Actually, we are planning a band together you can give a lesson or two on western music" Armi said, working on my suggestion.

"Sure, note it down" she said.

Armi noted the number down as fast as he could and re-checked it at least five times. I just couldn't believe this. As luck would have had it, Ayushi's dad was a lieutenant colonel serving the Indian Army and was posted in Agra. She was on vacation and was returning to Cambridge. She was a true 'Metallic Lady'.

Nizamuddin was nearing. We became good friends. Ayushi assured that she would definitely help us with the band. Armi assured that he would call her every once in a while.

"I think I have a crush on that girl" Armi whispered into my ears as we stepped out of the train.

I found it hard to believe. Armi had thousands of crushes but for some reason or the other he had found each one of them to be imperfect. Ayushi bade us goodbye and left for her destination.

It was a big day for me. Nizamuddin railway station was dear to me because of the endless crowd of teenage women. As I looked into their faces, I remembered that I too had a girlfriend. My phone beeped. It was Shreya. I picked up the call.

"Hello" I said.

"Do you have time to talk to me?" she said.

"Of course I have, but right now I'm at Delhi" I explained.

"One day you are busy completing assignments, the other day you are at Delhi; do you want me to believe you?" she said.

I remembered I hadn't talked to her for the last two days and she had every genuine reason to disbelieve me.

"If you do not have time for me than it's better if we do not talk again" she said, as I faintly heard a little whoop. She cut the line. I called her back but she wouldn't respond. I messaged her.

I m sorry, plz understand

Wll call u on reachin Agra bye, tc

We hopped into an auto rickshaw. "*Malviya Nagar, bhaiya*" Armi said.

Jerry opened the door. He was carrying his guitar. He lived in a rented two bedroom apartment.

"Welcome to Jerry's den" he said.

"Nice room" I said.

The room was in a complete mess. Magazines and newspapers were strewn all around. Two worn out sofas, a wrought iron bed and dining table and a brand new acoustic guitar adorned the room. As my eyes fell on the guitar, I was mesmerized by its beauty. It was an Aria. Although I had little knowledge about guitars, I could recognize the elite ones.

"That's an Aria Mac-45, isn't it? I asked as I sat in one of the old worn out sofas. Armi sat beside me.

"Yes, I bought that last Sunday" he said.

"Great. Oh! This is my friend Armaan, my roommate and the guitarist I was talking about" I said as I remembered to introduce him just in the nick of time.

"Hello Armaan" Jerry said.

"Hi! Jerry. Aria's are the best in business" Armi said, trying to be geeky.

"Yea, they are a class of their own" Jerry said.

"So, did you find a drummer?" Jerry asked.

"Yeah, I did find one. He lives here in Delhi" I said.

"Then why is he not here" he asked, puzzled.

I told Jerry the entire story about Mig and how I met him. He almost couldn't believe his ears.

"But I'm still not sure whether Mig will agree to be a part of our band. His life is at risk" I said.

"Don't you worry, we'll find a solution to that problem" Armi interrupted.

"There's an all India gig at Delhi next month and before that there are two more competitions at Agra. We can give it a shot there" I suggested.

"Band-It..?" I asked.

"Yep, Band-It" he answered.

"But we haven't practiced anything yet" I said.

"I'll think about it and inform you" Jerry said.

"In the meantime let's do one thing, let's record a song and see how we fare" Jerry said.

"Great idea" I exclaimed.

"Let's do a cover of Californication" Jerry said.

Fortunately, Armi had learnt the chords of this song and thanks to

Ayushi; he could play the bass quite perfectly. Jerry was apt at both acoustic and bass. The first trial was as worse as it could have got and Armi got almost all notes wrong. The second attempt was the worst and I thought Armi had indulged more in love talks than learning chords.

Finally, after six attempts, things seemed to take a turn for the better. The riffs sounded perfect although I suggested the duo to slow down the tempo. I joined in with the vocals and in thirteenth attempt, we recorded the song.

I played the record and it sounded almost the same as the Red Hot Chili Peppers themselves. Though we weren't the best, we had the potential to be the best.

The rest of the day, we spent musing over the past and how fate had brought us together. Mig hadn't agreed yet but I was sure that he would agree to be a part of our band.

Armi began counting his chickens before they even hatched and started planning about what he intended to do after attaining fame and he made me note them down.

1. Visit Aberdeen, the birthplace of Kurt Cobain.
2. Date Penelope Cruz- reason, he always fantasized about her.
3. Snorkeling in the underwater of the Great Barrier Reef.

All I could say was that it was eccentricity at its best.

The alarm sounded. It was 7:30. I set it back. There was still an hour to go before the GE class. It was strange that unlike everyday, Armi didn't wake me up. I jumped out of my bed, got out of my room and peeped in through one of the numerous windows in Armi's room. He was nowhere to be seen. It was strange. I called him.

"Fatass, where are you?" I said.

"Yamuna ghat" he said.

"What..? Are you crazy?" I asked, hoping that he hadn't lost his sanity.

"I thought of meditating before the big day" he said.

"Which big day ?" I said.

"Band-It" he answered.

Before he could say anything, I cut the line.

Mig had still not called me. I hoped that he was doing well. I dressed up and Armi arrived just in time for the GE class. In the middle of the class, I received a message.

Mig here, in Delhi

I felt better. I was worried about Mig and now that Nisha was back, I knew that he would definitely agree to be a part of our band.

In the afternoon, Mig called.

"Hi, Samarth" he said.

"Hi Mig, how was your journey?" I said.

"It tired me but I'm excited about my new job" Mig said.

"Decided on my band proposal?" I asked.

"Not yet, but I'll give it a thought tonight after talking to my boss" Mig said.

"Sure Mig, take your own time" I said and hung up.

I received a message.

hasn't had time to tok,

we r ending it

It was Shreya. I remembered I hadn't talked to her since the last two days. I called her back but she wouldn't pick up my calls. I tried over and over again but she wouldn't respond. I tried messaging.

Sorry, wanna talk

Messages failed. She was totally crossed. It was strange. On one hand, Mig had found his love and on the other I was losing mine. There was nothing I could do. I decided to take a nap.

I woke up perspiring. I checked out my watch. It showed 2:01 A.M. The same dream revisited me again. I had studied about dreams and their interpretations but I could not make out what my dreams meant.

The lights in Armi's room were still on. I wondered what he was doing at time hour of the night. I got off my bed and peeped in through the window. He was sitting beside the computer talking to someone over the internet.

I knocked on the door. He opened it and returned beside the computer in a jiffy. I was astonished.

"What are you doing at this hour?" I said.

"Shhh...." he signaled me to remain silent.

I peeked at his computer only to find him talking to Ayushi. Love was blossoming everywhere. I decided to leave him alone and returned back to my room. Sleep was a forgone conclusion. I called up Shreya again. Her cell was switched off. Guilt was killing me and I could do nothing about it. I decided to sleep.

The alarm sounded. It was seven in the morning. I decided to sleep more. No sooner had I closed my eyes, a loud bang on the door almost threw me of my bed. I got up and opened the door.

"I think you need an etiquette class" I said.

"Good news, thinass..." he said with a smile.

"I'm sleepy Armi..." I said, yawning.

"There's a college fest the next week and the semester results are out" he said.

On hearing this, I almost panicked. I had screwed up the previous semester and results at this time were unexpected. The next moment, I was sitting beside the computer, searching for my results.

"Roll no. BE6-1145" I filled up in a box and clicked enter. It was there. The web page was beautifully adorned with the mark sheet. I scrolled down the page. Armi counted the number of backs that I suffered.

"1, 2, 3…just 3.. I was expecting some more?" he said.

He was obnoxious to the point of agony.

"Shit, you still beat me" he said.

"How many backlogs did you bring" I asked.

"Four" he said.

Backlogs were piling up, love was rotting and my life seemed to be in a complete mess. The only solace I could fine was that Mig, Jerry and Armi were with me and at least I had an opportunity to give flight to my dreams.

All said and done, I decided to move forward and prepare for the fest ahead. I hadn't talked to Mig yet and we would need ample amount of practice before we could step on stage. I called up Mig.

"Hi Mig, Samarth here" I said.

"Hey, how's life"

"Not very good, would you like to play drums" I asked, coming straight to the point.

"Ahh…I don't think so, I mean, my boss won't allow me to take a leave now" he said. All the bosses in this world should be hanged.

"We need you…give it a shot" I said.

"Okay, I'll think about this" he said.

I wished him bye and cut the line. I prayed that Mig would somehow change his mind.

But I never knew that more surprises were in store for me.

Swadhya

Fests were nearing by the day. There were two gigs coming up. One was at our college and the other at a rival college. There would be two rock shows. Mig hadn't agreed yet and I had doubts if we would be able to compete in them. Time was running out.

Armi seldom woke me up now as he used to do earlier. He was getting busier by the day-with Ayushi, of course. They were 'good friends' now. I, on the other hand, wasn't talking to Shreya. The day before yesterday, we had a huge fight and now we were on the verge of breaking up. I had least expected this. My cell beeped. A message flashed on the screen.

Get ready

Dave Grohl's back.

It was Mig. He finally agreed to be a part of our band. I felt better. The first phase was over. I rushed to Armi's room to give him the news. He was still sitting beside the computer, wearing headphones, talking to Ayushi.

"International calls, huh?" I said.

"VoIP calls *zindabad*" he said, winking.

I left him alone, walked into my room and sat on a chair. We desperately needed funds-to buy drums or hire one. Without practice we were going nowhere. Armi entered into my room.

"How much does a ticket to London cost?" he asked.

"What? Have you gone nuts" I said.

"I think so" he answered.

"Great" I remarked.

"And I'm not going alone" he said.

"What do you mean by that?" I said.

"You are coming with me" he said.

For a moment, I felt excited but the next moment I realized that I didn't have a single penny to spend on a London trip.

"Where will the money come from?" I asked.

"Oh! Don't worry about that, I have got a brilliant idea" he replied

"And what about the passport and visa" I asked.

"*Mr. Jugaad hai naa...*" he said, as he popped a chewing gum in his mouth.

"Now, who's this Mr. Jugaad?" I asked, confused.

"Wait for sometime" he said as he closed the door and left.

I sank into the chair again. "*Wow London*" I thought. I wondered where he would get the money from.

I called up Jerry again. I wanted to tell him about Mig and that he had agreed to be our drummer.

"Hi! Jerry" I said.

"Hi! Samarth" Jerry said.

"Mig has agreed to be a part of our band and we have got a show at our college on Saturday night" I said.

"Great news" he said.

"We need some practice before the show but funds are posing to be a major problem right now" I said.

"Oh! Not a big problem, I can finance it for now" he said.

"That's great, thank you so much" I said.

"I'll be there on Thursday night. I will see you then" he said.

"Okay, bye" I wished him and cut the line.

The day was saved. I was proud to have Jerry as a band member. Slowly and steadily, all my dreams were coming true. I called up Mig to inform him about the show and he too readily agreed.

That evening Armi came back. He handed me two envelopes. I opened them and to my biggest surprise I found a passport and a visa in one and a British airways ticket in the other.

"We are leaving Sunday night" he said.

"Ah....ah, how did you get this?"I asked completely flabbergasted.

"A short story, I'll tell you later" he said.

I was very eager to know how he had managed get a passport and a visa and the money to buy a return ticket. I still couldn't believe I was going to London.

"What about the money?"I asked.

"Return it to me after you get a job" he said.

Thursday dawned. I woke up early. I couldn't sleep partly because I was excited for the upcoming adventures and partly because it had been more than a week I hadn't spoken to Shreya. I tried calling her but she wouldn't respond. Jerry and Mig could be here anytime and this would be our first show together.

Now we needed drums and a name for our band. I had thought of many names- Fate's children, Rock busters etc, etc but none of these names impressed me enough. I wanted something Indian, more precisely Sanskrit. I had never studied Sanskrit so I couldn't get any idea about the name. Nonetheless, I decided to propose these names in front of the members.

I still hadn't got off my bed and the devil arrived.

"Hey thin ass, had your breakfast?" Armi asked.

"Not yet" I said.

"Oh come on, you still haven't packed your bags" he said.

"Do you really love Ayushi?" I asked.

"I don't know" he answered.

"Then why go to London and waste such a huge sum of money" I said.

"Actually, there are a couple of reasons but before you ask, let me make it clear that I'm going to tell you only one of them, the rest are surprises" he said.

"Okay, tell me" I said.

"Actually, Ayushi has a dream. She would like her dream man to propose her with the Eiffel Tower in the background or in a Gondola in Venice" he said.

"Why London...?" I asked, confused.

"The rest are surprises" he said, winking at me.

As soon as Armi left, I had my breakfast and left for the college. I entrusted Armi with the job of picking up both Mig and Jerry. It was for the first time that the four of us would meet together under one roof.

I returned from college after completing all the formalities and to my utter surprise, I found Jerry at Armi's room. He had finally arrived. He brought with him his brand new Aria. Mig was yet to arrive.

I put forward the names that I had in my mind and I told them about the idea of keeping an Indian name for the band and everyone agreed. It was then, that Armi came up with the name Swadhya. I seemed to fit in perfectly. Swadhya meant self-work. After all, we had worked hard to come together to form our dream band.

My cell beeped. A message flashed on the screen.

Wll reach Agra in ten min,

pick me up

It was Mig. Half an hour later, Mig was sitting with us. I could feel the passion that was burning inside each of us. The hunger to achieve was immense. Everything was happening as I always wanted. We needed drums for Mig.

"Hey Armi, we need a drum set" I said.

"Don't worry mate, Mr. Jugaad hai naa..." he said.

I was desperate to know who Mr. Jugaad actually was.

Mig and Jerry had never seen the Taj Mahal before and we decided to visit the wonder. Armi was handed over the responsibility of finding a drum set.

"Wow! It's beautiful" Jerry said as he stepped into the archway.

"That's the reason it is one of the Seven Wonders of the World" I said.

"I hope to bring Nisha with me some day" Mig said.

My thoughts turned back to Shreya. We had shared so many moments- memories of which were hard to erase from memory.

"Let's have a photo together" Jerry said. Jerry clicked a photo. I looked at it. It was incomplete. Swadhya was a family and I wished Armi was here with us.

We wrapped up the visit as soon as I received Armi's message.

Got drums, see u at hostel

Mig was jubilant. He had found a new life. He would be playing on the drums after such a long time.

"Come on guys, let's start" I said.

"Just a minute Samarth, let me tune my guitar first" Jerry said.

"Which song do we play?" Mig said.

"I think it would be better if we play punk or funk rock because being first timers it will be easy for all of us" I suggested.

"I have played Californication once. The vocals and the instruments are easy" Mig said.

"And the music is entertaining too" Armi said, as he gave a pat on my butt.

"So Californication be it" I said.

"Come on guys, let's rock the town red" I said.

Amplifiers were plugged in and Mig took the drummer's seat. I turned on the microphone and the show started. Armi was playing the bass and had a hard time getting his tune right. After a few glitches, he finally got it right. The riff sounded perfect.

"Armi, slow down the tempo" Jerry said.

Mig began slowly but he soon caught up. The first trial was good although Armi wavered from his rhythm a couple of times. I wasn't sure about my vocals until Jerry appreciated me.

"It seemed Anthony Kiedis was singing" he said, as we finished our first jam-in session.

"Thanks" I said.

The second trial was even better. Armi grew in confidence and Jerry played the perfect riff. The song was coming out perfectly now.

"Once more" Armi shouted.

After seven more trials, we finally recorded our first demo. The sound quality wasn't good enough but it sounded just right.

"Good work, everyone" I lauded Swadhya.

"I'm done for the day, I think I need a drink" Armi said.

"Ok, we wrap up our practice for the day and I'll buy everyone a drink tonight" I said.

We headed for the same old M.K Bar. Armi was the happiest because it was only occasionally that I offered free alcohol and today was one of those rare days. I knew that the night could turn out to be my worst since Armi could guzzle down the entire bar if he wanted.

Nonetheless, I had saved enough money and I decided to go ahead with the risk.

Armi guzzled down twelve large mugs of beer and the three of us had a hard time carrying him off to the hostel.

Jerry and Mig arrived at the hostel early in the morning from the hotel in which they were lodged and we began our practice sessions. Armi arrived soon and he almost tipped over Mig and his drums. He had a huge hang over.

Now there was only one day before Swadhya would perform at its first ever gig. I found it hard to wait.

D-day arrived. The college looked colourful. This was the only day in a whole year when we could wear any attire other than the college uniform. I reinstated my spikes and Armi reinstated his age old Beetle shoes. Jerry wore a cap complementing his red Aria. Of the four, Mig was the best dressed. He wore a Reebok half jacket, faded jeans and a pair of sneakers.

Most of the bands had already arrived. In an hour, we would be on stage. I wanted to break this news to someone, someone special. I called up Shreya. She was the closest to my heart. I hoped she would pick up my call for once. I dialed her number. Fortunately, she responded.

"Hi, I wanted to talk to for sometime" I said.

"What is it?" she said. She was still angry.

"I'm sorry, I mean, I know I couldn't spare enough time for you but then...."

"But it's over, Samarth" she snapped me.

"I'm sorry, let these small things not come in between" I said.

"You don't understand, do you?" she said. It was getting worse now.

"I have to go now" she said.

"My dream has come true…I'm finally performing in my first show tonight" I said.

"Congratulations, bye." She cut the line. I turned around. Mig, Armi and Jerry were staring at me. I pretended to be fine.

"What happened? You look so numb" Armi said.

"There's nothing. Let's get on with our show" I said.

My heart ached, but I had to be strong. I couldn't have afforded to screw up my first gig. There were not many people watching but I was content with the way things were going. The day after tomorrow I would be in London.

The announcer announced our name. Swadhya would finally rock. We stepped into the stage. I watched the crowd. It was five hundred strong. We took our positions. I stood at the centre, Armi and Jerry stood at my left and right respectively and Mig just behind me.

A feeling of ecstasy crept inside me. I was scared at the first instance but slowly I gained in confidence. The crowd remained silent as we started. Jerry started the intro. The guitar sounded flawless. Soon, Armi joined in. As soon as I started with the vocals, Mig joined in.

Psychic spies from China
Try to steal your mind's elation
Little girls from Sweden
Dream of silver screen quotations
And if you want these kind of dreams
It's Californication

I completed the first stanza. The crowd still remained silent.

"Come on guys, I want you all to wave your hands high in the air"

I announced in the middle of the song.

No sooner I had announced it, the crowd got into their feet. They cheered every note that we played. I felt better. Swadhya was flowing. I could see Armi head banging.

The song ended on a perfect note and I could see the crowd waving and screaming. I was elated. Backstage, we hugged and congratulated each other. We had given our best shot and the results would tell the rest. We returned to the hostel.

I was exhausted. It was a hard day. Mig and Jerry returned to their hotel. Armi sat beside me.

"Broke up with Shreya?" he said.

"May be, may be not" I said with a shrug.

"Why didn't you tell me earlier?" Armi said.

"The problem wasn't that serious" I said.

"Everyone needs some time alone, may she need some time too" Armi said.

"Hopefully" I said.

"She will definitely come back and we have a flight to catch tomorrow, so pack your bags" he said, as he returned to his room.

I was dejected but I was optimistic. Sometimes when you love something, you need to set it free. May be, I had to set her free. I closed my eyes and turned back the pages of my memory. Amritsar flashed back, the Golden Temple, the silver Indica and the golden girl. Now, I only had dreams to comfort me.

The cock-a-doodle sounded. I checked out the time. It showed 7:00. All night I was dreaming, dreaming about me and Shreya in the British countryside, and enjoying the night sky, staring at the starry sky. All of a sudden, a demon like figure like appeared and gobbled me up.

Mig and Jerry as usual arrived early. We had planned to leave for Delhi together. I checked out my ticket. 11:30 P.M was the departure time.

"Hey thin ass" the devil called out again.

"What the hell is it now?" I said.

"Get ready fast, we have to leave in an hour" he said.

"Go to hell" I snapped him.

"Go to London" he said and left.

The next hour, we were in the train heading for Delhi. I was excited. I could only guess the surprises that would be in store for me. I had heard about the Buckingham Palace, the Thames, the London Bridge and the Piccadilly Circus and I had a hard time believing that we would be there the next day.

Reaching Delhi, we bade Mig and Jerry goodbye. There was still around nine hours before departure and we decided for some sight-seeing or more precisely lady-checking trip.

I had never seen an airport as large as the Indira Gandhi International airport. I wondered what Heathrow would be like. Boeing's and Airbuses were taking off and landing every few minutes.

"Did you call Ayushi?" I said.

"Of course not, dumbo...what's in a surprise then?" Armi replied.

"Will there be a television on the plane?" I said. I was curious since this was the first time I would be travelling in an international flight.

"British Airways is owned by my father-in-law and they will offer me a free laptop, a Durian bed and a personalized spa treatment" Armi said sarcastically.

After stringent security checks, we finally boarded the flight. Armi sat beside me and I saw him give dirty looks to an Indian airhostess who asked Armi to put on his seat belt.

"Her ass looks delicious, isn't it?" Armi whispered into my ears.

"You seem to have tasted thousands" I whispered back.

The plane took off. Mid air, I looked through the window. The sky was dark. I was waiting for it to turn blue.

A date in London..? Armi had gone nuts and so had I.

Metal in London

Heathrow airport, 5:30 am:

This airport was almost five times the size of the Indira Gandhi International airport. With escalators and swanky souvenir shops and restaurants, this airport had everything in it.

"Wow! It's beautiful, isn't it" I said.

"Of course it is. This is London" Armi said as he pulled his luggage from the trolley.

"Where do we put up?" I asked.

"Of course in a hotel dumbo" Armi said.

We hired a cab and drove through the picturesque expressway. The weather was dull and cloudy as I had seen in the numerous India-England cricket matches and a gentle breeze was blowing on our faces. I could faintly hear Armi singing to himself 'the Zephyr song' by the Red Hot Chili Peppers.

I had no idea what so ever where we were heading to. Armi was carrying with him a map and at periodic intervals he would peek at it and make strange faces which made me all the more confused. Forty minutes later the taxi stopped at Mig's command at Lexington Avenue.

"What now?" I asked.

"A soft bed and a hot shower await us" he said, pointing towards a three storied building across the street.

That was the very hotel where we had planned to stay. It was a three star hotel and entering inside I found the reception brightly lit with wonderful wall hangings.

Upstairs, a fully furnished room with wooden floors, including a coffee vending machine met our site. This was the very room where we would spend the next three days.

"Hey thin ass, I'll be back in an hour or two" Armi said.

"But where are you going?" I asked.

"Cambridge" he said, as he banged the door shut.

After a hot shower, I walked outside. The streets were neat and tidy and the number of Indian restaurants amazed me. The news was that chicken tikka masala had become the favourite dish of the British and I decided to take a bite at 'the Garuda's- a small but spacious restaurant adjacent to one of the London tube entrances.

The chicken tikka was delicious and every bite of the chicken melted inside my mouth and disappeared within no time. This wasn't very good particularly because I couldn't get the better of its taste and more so because of the fact that a single plate cost me 6.5 pounds, equivalent to five hundred Indian rupees. With that amount I could have gulped down an entire lamb in India. Nonetheless, it was a hearty meal and I decided to take a trip of the London Tube. I took a ticket to the Westminster Abbey.

"Armi, you have accumulated oodles of fat" Ayushi said.

"I think I need some exercise" Armi said, as he winked at her.

Ayushi looked as gorgeous as ever. Wallpapers of John Lennon, Paul McCartney, Pink Floyd, and Metallica adorned her room. A silver colored guitar and a Casio lay on the floor.

"Where is the Wembley arena?" Armi asked.

"A forty five minutes drive from here, but why are you asking that?" Ayushi said.

"We have to reach there by five. We'll pick up Samarth on the way. Now get ready and do it quick." Armi said.

"But what is there in the Wembley arena?" Ayushi asked.

"Don't worry, Ayushi, you will get to know once we reach there" Armi said.

Armi blindfolded Ayushi and within half an hour they were driving towards central London.

The Westminster Abbey, as I learnt is a gothic church in Westminster. I disliked gothic metal and I wanted to know if there was a relation between the two. I couldn't find any connection and it turned out to be the traditional place of coronation and the burial site for the English, the British and the monarchs of the Commonwealth. I wrapped up my visit to find something more adventurous.

I took the metro back to the hotel. It was almost five when Armi rushed into the room.

"Hey thin ass get down into that car" he said, pointing to a blue Ford through the window.

"What.... What happened?" I asked.

"Just come with me" he said and almost dragged me as I stumbled over two chairs and a table fan.

"Could you please tell me what has happened" I asked.

"Get inside the car" Armi said.

I was astounded to find Ayushi in the front seat, blindfolded and I was taken aback. *Was Armi kidnapping us for ransom or something*? I could only be a pessimist at that point of time. We were hurling through the street at a breakneck speed and I could only pray that Armi wouldn't mess this up.

Finally, after an express thirty five minutes drive we reached the Wembley arena. The giant white building greeted us. But the first thing that caught my eye was the giant Metallica poster. Just below it, written in bold letters was the line 'Live tonight'

Armi opened Ayushi's blindfold and pointed towards the Metallica poster.

"Oh! My God, I can't believe this" she remarked.

"I can't believe this too" I remarked.

Ayushi hugged Armi tight and I missed Shreya.

"Metallica is your favourite band, isn't it?" Armi asked.

"Yeah, It is" Ayushi answered.

"But why did you have to do all this?" Ayushi asked.

"I love you" Armi said.

"Oh! I love you too, Armi" she said blushing.

This time they hugged tighter and kissed in the middle of the street. Armi too had found his love. Armi handed us two concert tickets and we went inside the arena excited to see the legends of thrash metal playing for the first time in our life. Watching Lars Ulrich, Kirk Hammett and James Hetfield, the three of them together in one stage was once in a lifetime experience and a dream come true.

"That's great news" Jerry exclaimed in exultation as Mig had decided to shift with Jerry in his apartment.

"When are you shifting" Jerry asked.

"Tomorrow or the day after" Mig said.

"I'll be waiting" Jerry said.

"Bye Jerry" Mig said as he cut the line.

At the concert the crowd was enormous. The arena was jam-packed with around ten thousand fans. Kirk was at his usual best and James' vocals took my breath away. Ayushi and Armi were enjoying every moment. Metallica performed 'Nothing else matters' and the lyrics took me back to the times I shared with Shreya.

So close no matter how far
Couldn't be much more from the heart
Forever trusted who we are
And nothing else matters.

Three months ago, nothing really mattered. We were one. Things had changed and only time could heal the scars left behind. 'Nothing else matters' was the fourth song that Metallica played that evening and everyone was waiting for the final song with bated breath. It was 'Turn the page'. Every song seemed to complement the occasion. At that very moment, I decided to turn the page of my life. It pained but a new start would be better.

The song ended with a thunderous applause. Fans were screaming on top of their voices. I imagined myself in place of James Hetfield. I wanted to perform exactly like him. We came out of the arena rejuvenated. I had experienced one of the best moments of my life. We went for an autograph session. I got two autographs by James and Lars, Ayushi bought an audio CD and Armi bought a Metallica T-shirt.

It was eight in the evening when Ayushi dropped us at our hotel. Our first day was over and I would take some pleasant memories back home. There was just one more day before we would return to India.

"Bird's eye view of London, wow" Ayushi said as the London Eye reached its highest point. At the distant we could see the Thames winding its way through the city. Next on the list was the Tower of London.

"London Bridge is falling down" I sang as I clicked a photo of the beautiful piece of architecture. We wrapped our tour with a visit of the Buckingham Palace, the Trafalgar Square and the British Museum. Armi and Ayushi went on a date and I returned to the hotel.

"Wait, I'm coming in just a minute" Ayushi said as Armi was left stranded outside the door of her apartment.

"I can't wait much, I am hungry" Armi screamed as Ayushi closed the door behind him.

"Wait for a minute, you insatiable pig" she said.

After seven minutes of an agonizing wait, the door opened. Armi would have almost fainted and collapsed had it not been for the wall on which he was leaning.

Ayushi looked stunningly sexy. She was wearing a white shirt which acted more like a single-piece top. The shirt was almost transparent and Armi had a hard time guessing whether she wore anything under it. There was no trouser or the stilettos which she had been wearing moments ago. Armi, at the first instance thought he was hallucinating but soon realized that he hadn't taken any drugs.

"Come in now" Ayushi said as she tugged at his shirt and pulled him inside the room.

"Would you like to have some coffee?" Ayushi asked.

"Yeah, I think I would" Armi said.

"A hot cup of coffee can work wonders before you know what" Ayushi said, as she walked straight towards the coffee vending machine in the kitchen.

Armi said nothing. From the corner of his eye, Armi could see the delicate body that Ayushi possessed. It was a masterpiece. There were no scars, not a hint of them. It was for the first time that Armi was analyzing the intricacies of a woman's body. Armi turned on the audio player. The famous George Michel song 'Careless whisper' was playing on it.

Armi, like a silent predator entered the kitchen. She was still working on the coffee machine when Armi held her waist from behind. She took a deep breath and Armi turned her around.

"Naa…baby, coffee first" Ayushi said as handed over the mugs to Armi and made her way to the bedroom.

She put down the mugs on the table beside the bed and knelt down on her knees on the bed. Armi came after her. On the bed lay a copy of the Kama sutra. Armi quickly flipped through the pages and arrived at the chapter titled 'The missionary'

"This one" Armi said as he pointed it out to Ayushi.

"Come on baby" Ayushi said.

"You look beautiful" Armi said as he began unbuttoning her shirt. Ayushi looked straight into his eyes. The music changed from 'Careless Whisper' to Enrique's 'Addicted'.

Armi kissed on her lips and slowly moved down. For a moment Armi looked into her eyes. Ayushi unbuttoned his jeans and slid her hands inside. A cat mewed outside the window as both of them rocked to and fro.

Minutes later they lay over each other completely breathless.

"You are good, huh" Ayushi said, taking deep breaths.

"I love compliments" Armi replied, as he kissed on her navel.

"Will you marry me?" Armi asked.

"Of course I'll" Ayushi said.

Armi removed a thin strand of hair which was falling over her glowing red cheeks with his fingers and looked straight into her eyes.

"I love you and I always will" Armi said.

"I love you too" Ayushi said.

I was still waiting for Armi and Ayushi at the Heathrow. Armi had called me up saying he would be there within an hour or two. I checked out of the hotel and within forty-five minutes, I was at the airport. There was still one hour before departure.

Fifteen minutes later, I saw Armi accompanied by Ayushi entering the main restroom. They were walking arms in arms and looked like a perfect couple.

"Hey thin ass, sorry yaar" he said as he hugged me tight.

"It's fine. Hi! Ayushi" I said, pretending to see her to see for the first time.

"Hi! Samarth" She wished me back.

From the look on Armi's faces, I could say that the two had gelled together pretty well. It was time for our flight. Armi bade an emotional farewell to Ayushi almost on the verge of shedding tears. On the flight, he told me everything about what transpired between the two. I was amazed by the way kismet worked.

Then it was time for some dirty looks as I saw Armi trying to flirt with one of the Indian air hostesses who reciprocated him. An hour later, I fell asleep.

Agra, A day later:

I walked into the class. The teacher had not yet arrived. Everyone seemed to be staring at me. Armi was nowhere to be seen. I was wondering what I had done to attract such attention, when I heard the devil call me.

"Swadhya has won the Rock-o-Rolla" he screamed.

"I dashed out of the room and hugged him tight. I had tasted success in my first attempt.

In the director's room we were awarded shields and a cash prize. Deep inside, I thanked Shreya for being a part of my life. Without her I would never have visited Amritsar and would never have bumped into Mig and Swadhya would never have come into existence.

We went back to the class only to be welcomed with a standing ovation. Armi was enjoying every bit of his new found fame. I called up Mig and Jerry and congratulated them.

"I have shifted with Jerry" Mig said.

I was surprised at Mig's sudden decision but the reason he gave made me happy.

"There's an upcoming gig at a rival college" I said.

"We'll surely perform and win that too" he replied.

Focal Point

Jerry was eagerly waiting. It was 11 A.M but Mig had still not arrived. He had promised to be at Mig's apartment by 10'o clock. Jerry tried calling on his cell but it was switched off. A sense of panic gripped Jerry. He could find no reason why he was acting like a pessimist. He decided to wait.

Another hour had passed but there was no sign of Mig. Jerry was helpless. An hour later, he decided to visit Mig's apartment. He dressed up as fast as he could and took a cab straight to Mig's apartment. He knew that Mig's life was in danger because of his acute depression and his addiction to drugs. That was a major cause for worry.

On reaching his destination, Jerry found Mig's apartment door unlocked. He sensed that something terrible had happened. For once he decided to call the police, but ditched the idea at the last minute because that could arouse further problems because Mig had still not surrendered.

Opening the door slowly, he went inside. There wasn't any sign of struggle as all the furniture lay intact. But Mig was nowhere to be seen. A search in the bedroom and the kitchen yielded no results. The bathroom was the only place left. Inching closer, he opened the bathroom door and peeped inside. Mig was lying on the floor, unconscious, white foamy substance oozing out of his mouth. Jerry rushed inside and checked his pulse. It was still there. He was still alive. Quickly, Jerry called for an ambulance.

Forty five minutes later, they were at the hospital. Jerry completed the formalities. Doctors diagnosed a drug overdose but the worst was yet to come. Doctors couldn't say for sure whether he would survive. His condition was critical. An hour later his condition worsened and he had to be shifted to the ICU.

I was shocked on hearing the news. I just had my supper when Jerry called me up. By 11.30 P.M we were at the hospital in Delhi. All the time Jerry was with him doing everything the doctors told him too. He donated blood, brought medicines, food and even gathered a few people who would donate their blood. But there was no assurance that Mig would survive. I was tired after a hectic journey and I dozed off. All night I dreamed about the show in which Cobain appears and then disappears in a flash and the stage catches fire. This dream was repeatedly haunting me. This was some kind of premonition or I thought so.

It was exactly six in the morning when I woke up. All night I had been sleeping in the sofa, kept adjacent to the giant LCD television. Jerry and Armi were still sleeping. I walked up towards the ICU. Through the glass window, I could see Mig. He was sleeping peacefully. Various machines connected to different parts of his body was keeping him alive. I could only pray to the almighty.

The doctor came up from behind and put his hand on my shoulders.

"Will he be all right?" I asked.

"Hopefully" he said as he walked on.

I felt two other hands on my shoulders. It was Jerry. He hugged me as tears came flowing out of his eyes. I consoled him.

Armi walked up soon after. We sat at the canteen. Jerry hadn't eaten a morsel since yesterday. The three of us silently ate our food. The silence was killing me. I decided to break it.

"Doctors told me that Mig's going to be fine by Wednesday afternoon" I said, trying to be cheerful.

"Hopefully" Jerry said.

"Guys, my instincts tell me that he's going to be perfectly all right and we are going to win our next gig" Armi said, trying to follow in my footsteps.

We had just finished eating when the doctors called on us.

"Mig has regained consciousness" he said.

We felt relieved. "Can we meet him?" I asked.

"He is asleep at the moment. Wait for an hour and two and then you can talk to him" the doctor said.

An hour later, we were sitting beside Mig. Jerry narrated to him how he had found him unconscious and how he had brought him to the hospital.

"Thank you Jerry" he said.

"Not to mention" Jerry said.

"Doctors told you had suffered a drug overdose" Jerry said.

"I'm really sorry, I took methamphetamine. After all that I had gone through in my life this drug was the only thing that made me sleep peacefully" he said.

This shocked Armi. All his life he thought himself to be the ultimate drug addict. After all, alcohol is also a drug.

"Now you have to quit taking drugs" Jerry said.

"Definitely" Mig said.

Armi and I came out of the room leaving Jerry and Mig alone.

"Without Jerry, Mig wouldn't have survived" I said. Armi nodded. We entered the doctor's cabin.

"When can Mig leave for home?" I asked.

"Tomorrow, he needs another day's care" the doctor said.

Soon Mig was shifted out of the ICU. One more day and Swadhya would be together once again. We could win the next gig as well.

Classes were on and I and Armi returned to Agra late night. Mig had already recovered and Jerry would take care of him.

Next day, Mig was released from hospital and he vowed that he would never take drugs again. Mig shifted to Jerry's apartment and remained under his careful watch. Jerry was a guardian angel taking every possible measure to get rid of his drug addiction. Mig on the other hand threw drugs out of his life.

The gig at our rival college was approaching fast. We had to prepare another song for this. Mig had recovered fully and was ready to start anew. This time we would be pitted against Agra's best band, who for some reasons could not participate in the last gig which we had won. Also this gig allowed only metal to be played. In short, this would be the toughest competition we would be facing till now. This gig would test our talent.

Back in Delhi, Mig and Jerry were enjoying their days practicing at least five hours every day. Jerry taught Mig the basics of playing a guitar while Mig told him stories about his college life.

"I always wanted to be a part of a band" Jerry said.

"And now your dream has come true, hasn't it?" Mig said.

"Yeah, it has but I want to see myself playing alongside the likes of Mark Knopfler and Eric Clapton. They are icons" Jerry said.

"I idolize Cobain. I wish he was still alive" Mig said with a shrug.

"Did you tell Nisha about your encounter with death?" Jerry asked.

"Are you crazy? She will burn me alive if she comes to know that I was on drugs" Mig said, as he strummed Jerry's guitar.

"By the way, you never told me about your girlfriend" Mig said after a brief pause.

"I don't have one. My parents will find someone when time comes"

Jerry said.

"Why? Everyone needs someone to be at their side" Mig said, utterly taken by surprise that Jerry was still single.

"I have you" Jerry said.

For a moment, Mig was taken aback but he managed to hide his expression.

"Of course, I'm with you" Mig said, smiling at Jerry.

The Decibel was three days away. Such was Armi's passion that since the last three days he had locked himself up in his room and the only sound audible was the sound of the guitar. He was inexperienced and had never played metal before and he desperately wanted to learn playing Metallica to perfection. Ayushi helped him with the chords.

I called up Jerry.

"Decibel is on Wednesday" I said.

"We are arriving tomorrow" Jerry said. I cut the line.

I was confident that we would do well. But deep inside, I feared about competing against the best band of Agra. Nonetheless, there were three more days and we had ample amount of time to practice.

Jerry and Mig arrived early next morning. Mig recovered well enough and seemed excited about the new prospect. He loved to win. Armi was still sleeping when they arrived. He had been practicing all night long.

After an hour's rest, we decided to start practice. This time, Armi brought a larger drum set.

"This will cost us a thousand bucks a day but don't worry, it's free for us. Mr. Jugaad has done it again" Armi said.

Mig jumped in exultation on seeing the set of seven drums.

"Where the hell did you get this from? It consists of a bass, three rack toms, two floor toms, a snare drum, hi-hats and cymbals" Mig said as he explained the constituents. I was bamboozled by the terms he used. It was unfathomable.

"So, which song do we play?" I asked.

"Turn the page by Metallica" Jerry suggested.

"Nothing else matters" Armi said.

"I would prefer Mama said" Mig said.

"The organizer of this gig has asked every participating band to prepare a song by any metal band" I said.

"Let's do 'Nothing else matters'. It's a ballad and easy to sing for me. Only the guitar is a bit tough but Jerry can manage" I said.

"Let's do it guys" Armi said. We started the rendition. Half an hour into our practice, visitors arrived. They were none other than the *netas.*

Standing at the door were three guys. Dressed in kurta-pyjamas, they wore saffron scarves around their necks. I remembered that we were refused permission to practice at the hostel premises. The scariest thing about them was that they carried with them *kattas* or locally made guns. One of them called out Armi. He was the only one who could handle them with care. I didn't venture out because I didn't want my bones to be dismantled. But I prayed, for the *netas* of course. I prayed that Armi wouldn't smash their heads. Ten minutes had passed but I still couldn't guess what Armi was up to. Five minutes later, I heard some noises- a gun shot and sounds of running feet. Jerry and Mig were stunned. I walked out of the room only to find Armi with a gun in his hand walking straight towards me.

"They thought they would scare me" he said.

Armi acted like a stereotypical song and dance hero from a Bollywood masala flick who romances ladies in London and bashes the bad guys. But all's well that ends well. We went back to practice.

Amplifiers were connected and everyone took their positions. This was the first time that I was singing a Metallica. Although I had practiced the song a million times, singing live on stage was altogether different. Jerry started with the lead. Soon Armi joined in with the bass. I was surprised seeing Armi playing such a perfect tune. Practice does make a man perfect. Who could prove it better than Armi? All these days he was practicing Metallica with Ayushi's help.

I was happy with the trials. The record sounded almost similar to the original version except for the vocals. We wrapped our practice for the day. There was still one more day before the show down. Jerry and Mig left for their hotel while Armi and I stayed behind. No sooner had we finished our lunch, we heard sounds of gunshots outside.

"Armaan, come out of your burrow" a voice shouted.

Armi was outraged. He picked up a phone and dialed some numbers. He spoke for about ten seconds and then cut off the line. I was terrified. He walked out and I followed him. Outside, around twenty-five *netas* were waiting. They were armed with guns, knuckles and baseball bats. Armi was scared- I could say that when I saw his face turn pale but he managed to put up a brave face.

"Come on, you rascal, come down" another one shouted.

Thirty seconds later, I saw another twenty five bikes each with two people approaching the hostel premises. Everything stopped- the slogans, the abuses and even time. Armi smiled. It was then I realized that Armi had called in for support. It was that day when I came to know that Armi had a secret gang and this fact was kept well hidden from me.

The guys in bikes were armed with chains, rods, sledgehammers and weapons which could cause '*neta destruction*' if not mass destruction. The hostel emptied in a fraction of a second. Everyone seemed to be running for their lives. I could see Armi giggle.

"They will never come back again" he said, winking at me.

"You are no less a maniac" I said, winking back at him.

Once again the hero won the battle. Now we could practice our music in peace.

The next day, Jerry and Mig arrived early and continued late into the night. The clock struck eleven when we decided to wrap up our practice for the day. Tomorrow we would be on stage, battling it out against some of the best bands in Agra.

"The crowd was larger than it was in the previous one, isn't it?" I asked.

"Yeah, it is and we are next in line" Mig said.

We had prepared well. Mig, for the first time shed his disguise and regained his identity. Now it was Mriganka Saikia rather than Jaspal Singh on drums. GoD or the Generators of Destruction were playing. It was the best band in Agra and it was playing at home drawing huge cheers from the crowd.

It was show time. We stepped on stage. As usual, Armi stood on the left hand side of the stage while I took the centre stage. Mig sat just behind me while Jerry and his red Aria occupied the right. We looked photogenic.

Jerry started the lead. Twenty seconds later, I heard a loud cheer. The crowd was finding every second of the song 'Nothing else matters' irresistible since it was a soft ballad and had a large fan following. Almost everyone had heard this song. This strategy helped us. Wining did matter but what mattered more was the response and the response was amazing. Armi also joined in with his rhythm. I started the rendition.

So close no matter how far
Couldn't be much more from the heart
Forever trusting who we are
And nothing else matters

Never opened myself this way
Life is ours, we live it our way
All these words I don't just say
And nothing else matters

Trust I seek and I find in you
Every day for us something new
Open mind for a different view
And nothing else matters

"Come on guys, I want you all to sing with me" I shouted on the microphone. Mig was playing flawlessly and so was Armi.

Never cared for what they do
Never cared for what they know
But I know

So close no matter how far
Couldn't be much more from the heart
Forever trusting who we are
And nothing else matters

Never cared for what they do
Never cared for what they know
But I know

I continued. I was on a high. So were the other three. Armi seemed to be in a trance.

"Guys, I dedicate this song to my girlfriend, Shreya" I announced on the microphone.

I could see the crowd waving their hands high, in unison.

The song was ending and so was our moment of glory. This show was better than the first one. Jerry carried on with the lead.

So close no matter how far
couldn't be much more from the heart
forever trusting who we are
No nothing else matters

I ended the song with a loud growl. Armi, Mig and jerry continued playing the music. Few seconds later, I heard repeated shouts of 'once again'. I realized that we had turned the tide. We bowed and went backstage.

"Yeahhhh"... Armi shouted"

"What does your instinct say?" I asked Armi.

"We will win this" he replied.

An hour later alcohol was flowing. Cans of beer were opened. Celebration was on.

Results were announced the next day. Swadhya was invited to receive the honours. This was our second win on the trot. Next on our list was Band-It. It was the largest talent hunt competition for rock bands. Bands from all over the country participated to win the coveted prize- an album. In such a short period of time, we had reached the space and now were heading towards the stars.

"Is everyone ready for Band-It?" I asked, my head still heavy having not recovered from yesterday's hang over.

"Yeah!" the three roared.

"It's a month away. We need funds and loads of practice" I said

"We will conquer once again" Mig shouted.

Spirits were running high after our second win and now we thought we could conquer this world.

"You guys have to shift bases to Agra. That way, we can practice together everyday. Practice brings perfection and perfection brings victories" I said, looking at Jerry and Mig.

"But what about our jobs" Mig asked.

"You can get one here. Also living costs are not very high, so you can save enough" I suggested.

"Good idea" Jerry nodded, agreeing to my idea.

"I like this idea but my boss will hang me" Mig said. He was desperately trying to shake off pessimism from his brain.

"Screw your boss, so when are you guys shifting?" I asked.

I could see their shocked faces. Apparently, they were stunned by the pace at which I had altered their decision.

"Within a week or two" Jerry said. Mig's passion for rock could be seen. He agreed to screw his boss and get another job just to be a part of Swadhya.

"That's even better" I said.

It was final. Jerry and Mig were shifting to Agra. Early next day, they left for Delhi.

Band-It

The day finally arrived. The venue was Delhi. We hired a cab on a bright Sunday morning. We had practiced hard all these days. Armi was the happiest of the lot. Ayushi would be here too. Bands from all over India were pouring in slowly. In a short while, we would be there too. It was a six day long rock bonanza. Each day, we had to perform one song. Accordingly we had made a list of seven songs including an original piece. The song was 'When I held your hand', one of my own poems, which we had converted into a song with a few modifications. The music sounded somewhat similar to 'Rhythm of love' by the Scorpions, yet it was different.

Armi bought a brand new guitar for the event. It was a Fender and cost a fortune. The white and silver Fender instantly took my breath away. I had never seen one like this before. I felt ecstatic. This was the day I was always waiting for. Performing in one of the largest rock shows in India was my dream and this was coming true. Now I was waiting for something more-winning. The passion in Swadhya was something I had never seen before. Everyone was pumped up. I on my part took lessons on growling. You-Tube helped me.

The venue was as large as a football stadium with a crowd capacity of ten thousand. We headed straight towards the office where we registered our presence. We were scheduled for a performance later that evening. Then we headed straight to the hotel where lunch was awaiting us. Jerry seemed a bit tensed but Mig motivated him. Besides us, seventeen other bands from across the country were selected to compete against each other. The competition would be tough. To win this, we had to be tougher. The show would start exactly at six in the evening. All four of us went for an afternoon siesta.

Day 1:

The sun had almost set. Crowds were pouring in. I could see the various bands preparing for the battle ahead. The atmosphere was electrifying. But what caught my eye were the attires. People were wearing tattoos on their arms. Some had pierced eyes while others had piercing on their lips and tongues. Long hair was common among the band members. There was a girl band too. Dressed in minis they wore black lipstick and nail polish resembling Goths. I disliked Gothic metal. And girls- their shrieking voices irritated me to no extent.

I checked out the schedule. We were fifth on the list. Round 1 gave us an opportunity to play a song of our choice and that song was 'Fade to black'- a Metallica song. This song had melody, good lyrics and a heavy music. We had practiced this song around eighty times. We had perfected this song. The stage was almost triple in size than the one we had performed in our college. The lighting was incredible. The 40,000 watt sound system could knock out a person's brain.

Backstage, we met a couple of other bands. One among those was X-Trims. The band's lead singer was Sammy Matthews. It was a Goa based band. This band specialized in alternative rock. He seemed friendly. He smiled at me and I smiled back.

"Hi, Sammy Matthews" he introduced himself, as he came walking towards me.

"Hi, I'm Samarth Dasgupta, lead singer of Swadhya. These are my fellow members- bassist Jerry, rhythm guitarist Armaan Sharma and drummer Mriganka Saikia" I said as I introduced the trio.

"Hello everyone" he wished them.

Armi seemed disinterested while Mig and Jerry continued punching each other.

"So which song is your band playing?" I asked.

"We are playing 'Tears don't fall' by Bullet for my valentine" he said.

The show had started. There was a huge crowd, cheering every time a band stepped on stage and booing every time it played a note wrong. Three bands had already played and I could hear more boos than cheers. Next in line was Sammy's band. X-Trims had won numerous events including the runners up when title at last year's Band-It. They were desperate to win this year's title. I realized that we were pitted against one of the best bands in India.

A huge roar went up from the crowd when X-Trims stepped on stage. They were a recognized lot and the generally merciless crowd showered some respect to the band. A feeling of nervousness gripped me. I revised the lyrics once more. Armi was strumming on his guitar.

Ten minutes later, X-trims stepped out of the stage. They were satisfied with their performance. It was time for Swadhya to showcase their talent. We stepped on stage. The audience welcomed us with a loud boo. I was expecting this. It did get into my nerves but I managed to keep my cool.

We took our usual positions on stage. Jerry started on his lead.

"Ladies and gentlemen, this is Swadhya, performing the cover of 'Fade to black' by Metallica. The judges looked uninterested. I could see one of them frowning. Perhaps they perceived us to be one of those low graded bands.

Thirty seconds into Jerry's lead, Armi joined in and an eerie silence crept over the stadium. Mig joined in and then I started.

Life it seems, will fade away
Drifting further every day
Getting lost within myself
Nothing matters no one else
I have lost the will to live
Simply nothing more to give
There is nothing more for me
Need the end to set me free

Things are not what they used to be
Missing one inside of me
Deathly lost, this cant be real
Cannot stand this hell I feel
Emptiness is filling me

Suddenly the stadium erupted into huge cheers. This was what I was waiting for all my life. I could only savour the moment. I looked at the judges as I plucked out the microphone and shifted my position to Jerry's end. Armi was jumping up and down. Mig was at his best. I continued.

To the point of agony
Growing darkness taking dawn
I was me, but now he's gone

No one but me can save myself, but its too late
Now I cant think, think why I should even try

Yesterday seems as though it never existed
Death greets me warm, now I will just say good-bye

Swadhya had clicked. Five minutes later, the song ended and we exited the stage with a huge round of applause.

Day 2:

We had garnered the maximum points on day one. Our closest competitor was X-trims. The best was yet to come. It was our second day and we had to play a song chosen by the judges. This round was the toughest of all and could decide a band's fate. The four of us sat together and were discussing a strategy when we heard a knock on the door. Armi opened it. It was Ayushi. She jumped over him. I thought she didn't notice us. Seeing us, she quickly got back on her feet.

"I'm sorry" she muttered, visibly ashamed at the way she had behaved. Armi introduced her to Jerry and Mig.

"Welcome to the world of Swadhya" I said.

For the next three hours, we sat down, discussing our plans on how to tackle the judge's choice round.

It was show time once again. X-Trims one once again, entered the stage with a rousing reception. This was the only band which could pose a danger to our winning chances. I could hear the judges announcing 'Cowboys from hell', a song by Pantera which I had never heard off. The judges gave a band three options out of which a band had to play one. This was particularly dreadful because the judge's choice of songs were mostly unheard off by me. A failure to sing anyone of the three could even lead to disqualification. We couldn't have prepared any song for this round and I wished I knew some bookies would have fixed it for us. This round was almost similar to an engineering exam. No matter how many 'pharrahs' you had, if a question popped in from out of the syllabus, you had no other option than to leave it. None the less, I decided to put up a brave fight.

X-Trims exited the stage and it was time for us to display our talent to the world. We took our positions. The judges announced their first option- Dead memories by Slipknot. I was expecting this- a song by some unknown band, though Slipknot was quite famous.

"Can I have the next option please?" I said.

The next option almost knocked my brains out. It was a song by Megadeth. Although I knew the song, I couldn't have sung Dave Mustaine nor could Armi have played its rhythm. I thought I was screwed.

"Next option please" I said. This was our last opportunity. I prayed hard.

"Can you sing 'Territory' by Sepultura?" one of the judges asked me.

Luckily, we had practiced this song a couple of times. Also we had no other option left. I discussed it for a couple of minutes with the trio.

"Yes Sir, we can" I said, as Jerry started on the lead.

I realized that that the first note had terribly gone wrong. I could see Armi perspire. Only Mig seemed confident. I started. Expectations had risen and the crowd became silent. I thought we could have carried on until Armi screwed it up. He stopped playing mid way. He had probably forgotten the chords. Jerry covered up but it wasn't enough. Slowly, I could hear my voice drain out. Loud boos went up from the crowd. There was palpable tension on Jerry's face. I signaled him stay calm but it was over by then. The judges had already disqualified us. We exited the stage leaving behind the loud booing sound.

At the end of the show, I checked out the rankings and the points. X-Trims had leapfrogged us to occupy the first slot. We were lagging behind at a distant seventh. We could not garner a single point from this round. Swadhya seemed disillusioned but I had made up mind to make a comeback.

Day 3:

Ayushi hugged Armi as we entered the stadium. She would be watching us performing. The third round allowed us to perform a song of our favourite genre. Grunge was a unanimous decision. We had practiced 'Smells like teen spirit' a hundred times. It was said that even the great Cobain had a hard time singing this song. Though not perfectly, I learnt to sing it almost to near perfection.

Everywhere, I could see the bands preparing their songs. The Gothic all girl band was the 'Gothomorics'. They were an ugly lot. They reminded me of Marilyn Manson doing a stage show in bra and a mini skirt. I headed straight for the toilet. The toilet seemed different from the one I had visited the day before yesterday. Maybe, it had been refurbished. It was almost empty except for some closed doors and red lights flashing with an occupied sigh in them. I went inside one of the empty cabins and sat down in one of the European styled ones. After five minutes of a brain storming session, I came out only to receive the biggest shock of my life. One of the gothic girls stood right in front of me, her back towards me. She hadn't seen me yet and I realized that I had entered into the ladies' toilet. I slowly turned back and was about to bolt when I felt a soft hand latch me from behind. She held me and refused to let me go. She pushed me against the wall and slid her hands inside my shirt. I could feel her breath on my face and her sharpened nails on my tummy. I was horror-stricken. She looked like a vampire ready to suck all the blood out of my body.

"Do not fear, I'm not going to eat you but I can lodge a complaint against you for trespassing" she said.

"Please don't do that, I can clarify" I said.

"Kiss me or die" she said.

I looked at her black lips for a while. A piercing on her tongue almost freaked me out.

"Aww...I can't" I said as I tried to free myself off her grip.

"You won't kiss me, will you?" she said.

I took a deep breath and was about to make another attempt to run.

"Stand right there or else I complain" she said, as she washed her face.

I stood right there like a prisoner bound in a long chain. A few seconds later she turned back at me. Her lip colour was gone and the enormous amount of makeup that she had put on disappeared. She opened her hair. I was mesmerized by her beauty.

"Do I look like a vampire to you" she said, still upset at the way I had behaved.

"Of course not. You look beautiful" I said. A little bit of flattery does help sometimes.

My cell beeped. I picked up the call.

"Thin ass, where are you? We have to be on stage within a minute" Armi said.

"I will be there in a minute" I said as I cut the line.

"Hi, I'm Samarth, lead singer of Swadhya" I said as I introduced myself continuing from our earlier conversation.

"I'm Megha, lead singer of the Gothomorics" she said.

"I'll see you after the show" I said as I rushed out only to find Mig and Armi frantically trying to find me.

"What the hell were you doing in a ladies toilet?" Armi asked, completely taken by surprise on seeing me coming out of the ladies toilet. Adding more fire to the speculation, he saw Megha exiting the toilet.

"Oh, now I understand. Instead of practicing you were tom-toming with a Goth" he said. I saw Mig smile. I smiled back and the three of us joined Jerry. I stole a glance of Megha. She had transformed into a Goth once again.

We entered the stage. X-Trims had just played 'My sacrifice' by Creed. They were consistently performing well. Fortunately, the crowd was more disciplined that day.

"Ladies and gentlemen, tonight we are performing the Rolling Stones number nine song of all times 'Smells like teen spirit' by the legendary band Nirvana" I announced.

As soon as I had completed, Jerry started on the lead. It was a lively song and the teenage crowd almost loved it instantly. The song required a special talent. Even an experienced singer could falter singing this song. Soon, Jerry and Mig joined in.

Load up on guns bring your friends
Its fun to lose and to pretend
She's overboard my self assured
I know I know a dirty wor
Hello, Hello.....

With the lights out it's less dangerous
Here we are now
Entertain us
I feel stupid and contagious
Here we are now
Entertain us
A mulatto
An albino

A mosquito
My libido
Yea

The crowd loved it. I could see the teen spirit in them.

"Guys, I want everyone to create a pit with the girls at the centre and I want everyone to move in a circle" I announced as I remembered seeing a show of a very famous band in which the lead singer does the same thing.

No sooner had I announced it, I saw a huge pit with the girls at the centre and around fifty guys circling it. People were hopping and tripping over each other as they cheered every note that I sang. The output was exceptional. It couldn't have got better than this. I continued with the song.

I'm worse at what I do best
And for this gift I feel blessed
Our little group has always been
And always will until the end

Hello, Hello......

With the lights out it's less dangerous
Here we are now
Entertain us
I feel stupid and contagious
Here we are now
Entertain us
A mulatto
An albino
A mosquito
My libido

Yea

And I forget
Just what it takes
And yet I guess it makes me smile
I found it hard
It's hard to find
Oh well, whatever, never min

Hello, Hello....

As I sang the last few lines, my voice got drowned. I could hear the audience sing. Even the judges were overwhelmed by the response. I could recognize the expression on their faces. Swadhya returned with a bang. Swadhya stole the show.

We stepped out of the stage. An hour later the show ended. Swadhya had won the round. From the seventh position, we jumped to the second place. We were now lagging behind X-Trims by a mere three points. We still had a chance.

Backstage, Ayushi rushed in and hugged Armi. Everyone stared at the two but Armi never cared. This was exactly what he wanted- an image of a rock star.

Day 4:

The relaxed ambiance of the restaurant I had chosen for my first date with Megha was the most expensive I had visited till now. Megha could be here anytime. The waiter decked up the table with a rose and lots of rose petals at my direction. Since it was my first date with Megha, I had ordered custom made chocolate brownie with a scoop of cranberry jelly as I slowly felt the weight of my wallet dwindle. Finally, she entered. She looked elegant in a combination of white kurti and blue denims with matched 'jootis'. Her piercings were gone and instead of the black lip gloss, she put on light maroon. Her gothic identity had totally disappeared.

She came straight towards my table and sat down facing me. I could smell her perfume. It was intoxicating.

"You are looking gorgeous" I said leaning forward, almost whispering into her ears.

"Thanks and congratulations" she said.

"Which song are you performing tonight" she continued.

"Tonight we will perform 'Please don't cry' by Guns and Roses" I said.

"I'm amazed by the way you guys perform. Swadhya doesn't look like it's an amateur band." she said.

"It's because we generally go for songs keeping the Indian audience in mind and let's not talk about rock. Tell me something more about you" I said.

"Born in Delhi, brought up in Delhi, studying in Delhi, sang and performed in Delhi, three ex-boyfriends in Delhi" she said.

"Phew! That was one hell of a profile" I remarked.

She had a great sense of humour. There was certain magnetism about her personality, an aura which I could feel when talking to her. The chocolate brownie arrived and as the waiter put the plate down on the table I remembered the rose I had bought for her. I picked up the rose and offered it to her.

"Wow! Rose!" she exclaimed. "Is this for me?" she said, taking the most seductive flower according to me.

"No, it's for the Goth inside you" I said. She laughed. I tried to see Shreya in her. I failed. She was long gone. I thought I couldn't love anyone more than her. Amritsar flashed back. I could feel something in my eyes. They were getting moist. I could see Megha examine the rose. I quickly wiped my tears away. Men aren't supposed to cry. I had prayed endlessly for my love, even made a secret trip to Fatehpur Sikri. "Maine mannat mangi hai" I said without being aware of Megha's presence.

"What?" she said.

"Ah! Nothing" I said.

"You are crying, aren't you?" she said.

"Men don't cry" I said trying to sound funny but I was overwhelmed by the sudden surge of emotions. Megha grasped my hands tightly.

"Past has passed" she said. How did she know about it?

"Tell me everything" she said. An hour later I was crying like never before. People stared but I just couldn't refrain myself from shedding tears. We came out of the restaurant and Megha embraced me. *Is she the one?* But I feared treading towards love once again. I feared of losing it yet again.

It was almost show time when I entered the green room. Jerry and Mig were pumped up. I entered inside with Megha arms in arms with me. Armi was perplexed and so was Mig.

"I'll see you after the show" she said as she left. I needed a hand and Megha lent me an arm.

The lights went out as Swadhya entered the stage. This was a part of our performance. The garrulous crowd was puzzled. It was time for some love ballads. In the ensuing darkness that had engulfed the stadium, the sound of Jerry's guitar echoed throughout. 'Please don't cry' was one of my all time favourites. No sooner had Jerry finished the intro, Armi joined in and the lights flashed back. The crowd roared and I could hear the deafening sound of my voice blaring out of the sound system. I could see one guy holding a burning lighter in his hand and waving it in the air. Slowly, others too joined in. At the end of the song I could see a vast sea of burning lighters which stretched at least to a quarter of a mile. This was something I had never expected. Swadhya had taken the lead again. But then, there were two more rounds to go.

Day 5:

All night I couldn't sleep. Swadhya was slowly inching towards its hour of glory. Megha on her part had hijacked my mind. Today we had to perform any song from the 70's. It was an easy choice as we had practiced 'Hotel California', the most popular song by the Eagles to perfection. I woke up early. I checked out my watch. It showed 8:30. The other three were still sleeping. X-Trims were also lodged at the same hotel. I saw Sammy Mathews practicing on his guitar. I went over to him.

"Practicing hard, huh?" I said.

Sammy continued playing. He seemed troubled. "Hi, preparations going on in full swing?" I said, this time a bit louder.

"Oh! I'm sorry, I didn't notice you" he said. He was acting weird. There was something wrong about Sammy. He seemed uninterested. May be he feared losing the title once again.

"Which song are you playing tonight?" I asked.

"I don't know, we haven't decided yet" he said.

"See you then" I said, as I went back to my room.

Entering inside, I found Megha sitting on a chair reading a copy of the Rock Street Journal.

"Congratulations" she said.

"Why?" I asked.

"Swadhya is on Rock Street" she said.

"What?" I said, completely taken aback. I grabbed the magazine from her and flipped through the pages as fast as I could. I arrived at page number 46 and there it was- a photo of Swadhya under the headline 'Bands to watch out for'. I quickly read the article below. I could merely believe it. Swadhya was voted the best debut band and we were also touted to be the winners of Band-It. I realized why Sammy was disappointed after all. X-Trims were on the verge of losing this years title too. I ran out to give the news to the other three. I was shell shocked on entering Armi's room. The three were already celebrating. Beer cans had already been opened.

"Hey, where have you been? We have been searching for you" Armi said. I stood there watching.

"Come in now, it's celebration time. We are on Rock Street Journal" he said. Megha pushed me from behind and then she cuddled me. I was overjoyed. My dream had at last come true. Armi and Mig poured beer all over me and Megha. I joined in with the celebration.

I was feeling dizzy. We had crossed almost all the hurdles but there were still two more to go. Megha turned herself into a Goth once again but this time to my utter surprise, I found her beautiful. I wondered if I were in love. I hadn't told her anything yet and never thought about it until Jerry came up to me.

"You love her, don't you?" he said.

"I don't know for sure. Butterflies do fly inside my stomach but the intensity isn't like the one I had when I fell for Shreya" I said.

"I'm pretty sure she loves you" Jerry said.

"I know she does" I said.

"Then go ahead mate" he said. My fuzzy brain had stopped working. I decided to tell her at that very moment. May be she was expecting it after all. I called out Megha. She came running in.

"Would you like to be a part of my life" I asked.

"I am a part of your life" she said, holding my hands tightly. Her statement almost made my heart skip a beat.

"I'll be back after my performance" she said. I stood still as I watched her go. It was crazy that I had fallen in for a Goth, but she was more than a Goth. She was gem one could treasure for the whole of his life with the utmost care. I went back to the trio. Everyone was fired up for the night's performance. I signaled Jerry that everything had gone smooth and Megha had accepted my proposal. I revised the lyrics once more. There was still an hour to go before our penultimate performance. I went back to the green room. The view almost knocked the living daylights out of me. Some one had smashed Armi's guitar. Jerry's guitar was missing. Some one had stolen it to prevent us from performing. I picked up Armi's wrecked guitar and rushed out. The trio was stunned when they saw me holding the smashed guitar.

"Who did this?" Armi said as he came running towards me.

"I don't know. I just saw it" I said. Armi was fuming.

"Where's mine?"Jerry asked.

"Bad news, it's missing. Only the drums have been left intact" I said. Mig heaved a sigh of relief.

"How much time do we have" Mig asked.

"Half-an-hour" I said.

In half an hour, we had to hit the floor and at this crucial juncture someone had screwed us up. I suspected Sammy behind this. He didn't seem very happy with the way Swadhya was performing.

Luckily Megha arrived just in time and saved the day for us. I told her what had happened and she offered her guitar to Armi. Now, we needed another one. The host announced the name of X-Trims. I saw Sammy give an angry look before entering the stage. Friends had turned to foes.

X-Trims performed well as usual. I registered a complaint with the concerned authorities about our missing instruments. They compensated us by providing a spare guitar. Armi was dissatisfied.

"I'll kill that bastard if I lay my hands on him" Armi said. Deep inside I knew who had conspired against us. It was none other than Sammy.

It was time. We stepped on the stage. In this round audience would choose a song for us. As luck would have had it, Swadhya got a song of its choice-'Romeo and Juliet' by Dire Straits. It was a soft romantic rock n roll song and I enjoyed singing it.

"Folks, I dedicate this song to Megha, one of my best friends I announced before starting.

Jerry was at his usual best. At a distant, in the midst of the crowd, I recognized a face. It was Megha. She was smiling away at me. I smiled back at her.

The song lasted four minutes and thirty-eight seconds to be precise. Once again, the audience applauded us and we exited the stage with a standing ovation by the judges themselves. We were one step away from winning Band-It. I checked out the points table. We had taken an unassailable lead. Outside the green room I heard a commotion. Sammy Matthews was arguing with the police. Soon, he was cuffed and led away. Megha arrived from behind.

"The CCTV cameras recorded Sammy destroying and stealing your stuff" she said. X- Trims was disqualified and disgraced.

Armi came in from behind and poured two cans of beer over me. Jerry and Mig joined us and we huddled together as we celebrated the night. Swadhya had come from nowhere and won the biggest rock competition in the country. That night, I slept well.

Day 6:

With X-Trims disqualified, no other band could match Swadhya's prowess. This was our last day. I had prepared my most beautiful composition. It was a love ballad. I had prepared this keeping Shreya in mind. The last round allowed only original compositions to be played.

Armi was celebrating. Beer cans were strolled all over his bed. He drank a record shattering 23 cans of beer in a single night. Armi was still asleep when Ayushi knocked on the door. He woke up with a jerk and opened the door. His eyes were still shut when Ayushi handed him a guitar. Armi was overjoyed as he held the red and black Fender.

"A gift for doing so well" she said.

"Thank you so much" he said as he led her inside the room. Armi played the song 'You are not alone' by the Eagles dedicating it to Ayushi.

Watching the sunset, sitting in the lush green lawn beside the India gate, hand in hand with Megha was pure romance. I could see her twinkling eyes scanning the horizon as we spent the evening sharing funny anecdotes, discussing our favourite bands and arguing with an ice-cream vendor for mixing chocolate flavor with black current. We returned for Swadhya's final performance just in time.

After the exit of X- Trims, Swadhya's probability of winning Band-It had become hundred percent. More precisely Swadhya had achieved its glory.

Backstage Mig and jerry were waiting for us. Armi hadn't arrived yet Megha left me and joined her mates.

"Are we ready?" I asked

"We are fucking ready" Mig said. Abuses now had become a norm.

Armi arrived just in time. Seven minutes later we stepped on stage. This was the last day and Band-it had registered the biggest turn up. I sat on a chair at the centre of the stage.

"Folks, tonight I'm gonna play my own composition. I had written it for a very special person who is not in my life now" I said. The crowd went silent. I could hear whispers all around.

Jerry started with the lead.

When I held your hand, the sun shined
Murky waters glistened, I was overjoyed,
Ecstasy crept in, nothing else mattered,
Still remember the day, I was in tears

When I held your hand, our hearts came closer
In your mystifying eyes, I helplessly wandered
And as I danced to the tunes of love,
There were moments I truly savoured

Cho: Baby, where are those days
When under the shade we danced
Baby where are those days
When under the moon light we prayed

"For all those who do not believe in love or have never experienced its aura, experience it, it's beautiful" I announced in the middle of the song as the music continued blaring. I had never seen as silent a crowd before. Most of the faces were grim. I succeeded in doing what I wanted- make everyone cry.

When I held your hand, I said a silent prayer,
That we would be together and together, forever
You gave me a reason to smile,
Enriched my life and made it worthwhile

And as I still hold your hand
And walk over the golden sand,
I make a promise; I'll hold your hand
And walk a thousand miles till the end....

The song ended. Mig and Jerry displayed their prowess on drums along and guitar respectively. After three minutes of a heart breaking rendezvous, the audience enjoyed every bit of the instrumental played by the two.

The show ended and we went backstage. The judges showered us with heaps of praises. "Swadhya would one day be the emperors of rock" one of them commented.

But the journey of rock was still to be completed. We had a long way to go. An album was just the beginning.

Hanover, Germany:

Klaus Maine was watching a recorded video tape of the India's newest bands. He was the lead singer of the Scorpions. They had made up their minds to tour India.

"Pretty interesting" he said, as he handed the tape to his manager.

"Tell the organizers in India" he said.

I had no idea whatsoever that in the coming months, one of the world's leading bands with an iconic status and a cult following would invite us to perform along with them.

Opening for the Scorpions

Three weeks had passed but the celebration was still on. Our debut album was in the making. Semester exam was approaching and I had spent my days composing songs rather than collecting notes. I was busy writing lyrics for two new songs which would grace our album. In addition to these two, we had managed to compose music for my older poems. Mig and Jerry returned to their respective jobs. Armi had almost burned out, courtesy the umpteen number of beer cans he had gulped down in the last few weeks. We were showered with an unprecedented amount of praise in the college. We were now stars.

Armi was enjoying his new found star status. Even Miss Tanya, who had once chided him for his you-are-a-wild-cat statement, now showered tons of praises on him. She seemed to have a crush on Armi. In the college, he would strum his guitar and entertain girls. He had become every girl's dream boyfriend. He had grown his hair, almost shoulder length and pierced his chin. Tattoos of vampires and blood sucking bats graced his arms. The transformation was amazing. But the egotist in him never faded. He had almost ripped the guts of a *neta* for his '*saala*' remarks. He had to he rushed to a hospital. No wonder, Armi was handed a three day suspension.

Three days prior to the commencement of the semester exams, Mig came in to visit me. He looked gloomy. Apparently, he was wary of something. He was trying to throw drugs out of his life but the addiction was impossible to overcome.

"Nisha has threatened to leave me if I do not leave drugs" Mig said. He had lost much weight and he looked sick.

"I do not want to lose her yet again" he said. Insecurity was killing him.

"The more I think about it, the more I fear" he continued.

"Lately, my thoughts have turned towards Shrejas; I dream about him every single night" Mig said.

"Is there any solution?" Mig was exhausted. He was tired with the life that he was living.

"It's complicated" I said, after listening to his account.

My mind almost stopped working. I was no psychologist and it was an altogether new thing for me and there was no way I could have helped him with advices and suggestions.

"I'm ashamed of myself" he said.

Apparently, guilt was killing him. He held himself responsible for Shrejas' death.

"You are a human. Humans tend to slip. There is nothing to be ashamed of" I said consoling him as he sobbed. The guilt was killing him. The only thing I could have done at that point of time was to get rid of his guilt. I had heard about a similar case where the guy committed suicide. He didn't seem suicidal but guilt does drive one crazy.

"I love Nisha. I fear she would leave me alone again. What do I do?" he said, as he wiped his tears. He had put the most difficult question in front of me.

I had no answer. "Everything will be fine" I said. Mig left.

On the last exam day, I received a call.

"The Scorpions is touring India next month. Would you like to open the concert for them?" the voice on the other side of the phone said.

I was numbed. Opening for the Scorpions? I could hardly believe it.

"Definitely we would like to open the show" I said without thinking twice.

This was the most exciting prospect for Swadhya. The Scorpions were known for their hit songs 'Rock you like a hurricane' and 'Winds of change' and enjoys a cult following across the world.

"They are performing at Delhi, Mumbai, Bangalore and Shillong. Your band has been shortlisted for performing at Shillong" the voice said.

"Sure, we would be happy to perform there" I said.

"You have to come to Delhi for an audition on Monday" he said.

"Definitely, we would be there. Thank you" I said, as I noted down the address. I wished him good bye and cut the line.

Shillong was my second home after Guwahati. Performing at home in the midst of pine trees and the blooming jacaranda flowers along with one of the most popular bands of all times would be a dream come true.

I quickly called Armi, Jerry and Mig and gave them the news. Within minutes Armi came rushing in. "Are we visiting Shillong?" he asked.

"Yes, we are" I said, confident enough that we would crack the audition.

"Wow! Scotland of the East, we are coming" he remarked. He was more excited at the prospect of visiting Shillong than the fact that we would perform along with the legendary Scorpions. Mig was happy too. It would almost be a year since he would be visiting home. Nisha was eagerly waiting for his return. She was one proud girlfriend.

On a dull and cloudy Monday morning, we hired a cab to Delhi. We were confident that we would clear the audition. Megha would be waiting for me.

The auditions had already started when we reached there. A few Europeans were also present. Quickly, we were led to the recording room where we recorded two compositions- one from our soon to be released debut album and the other being 'Winds of change' by the Scorpions themselves.

After few minutes of a break, one of the Europeans, who he had introduced himself as Thomas Ernst Klett came up to me. He had a towering personality. Even Armi had a hard time looking up into his eyes.

"Are you sure you can perform alongside Scorpions" he said in a German accent.

"We are very much confident about that" I said.

"Then congratulations, you are in" he said. Mig leaped up in joy as he heard the news.

Wednesday dawned. I was very eager to perform in front of the home crowd although dad was crossed with me for having indulged in music more than my engineering. Nonetheless, I went ahead and invited him for my first concert at Guwahati. As expected, he flatly refused my invitation. There was still five days before the concert and we had decided to start practicing from this day.

Breaking norms, Armi woke me up after a long time. I checked out my phone only to find seventeen missed calls and a message. It was Jerry. I sensed that there was something wrong. I read the message.

Mig hasn't been home since yesterday
Need you here urgent

I dressed up as quickly as possible and reached Jerry's apartment. Mig had disappeared. My worst fears were coming true. I could only hope that he hadn't committed suicide.

"He isn't picking up calls since yesterday night" Jerry said.

"I think we should lodge a report with the police" I suggested.

"I had called up his office but they said that he left at his usual time which is 9:30 yesterday night" Jerry continued.

It was twelve hours since Mig was last seen and I understood that the problem was serious. It was finally decided that a missing report be lodged with the police. An hour later we were at the police station. Armi had also arrived. We lodged a report and went back to Jerry's apartment. We could only pray that everything would be all right.

I woke up with a jerk. I opened my eyes to find Jerry and Armi shaking me violently. I had no idea when I had fallen asleep.

"Mig has been found" Jerry said. I could faintly hear his voice.

The dream had raised its ugly head again. When I first had this dream, there were three guys on stage including me. The dream I had just now, also had three. The fourth one- the drummer was never there. I believed in prophesies and premonitions but I never paid heed to these paranormal beliefs. But I could sense that there was some relation between my dream and Mig's disappearance.

"Come on Samarth, wake up quick. We have to be at the hospital" Armi screamed.

I woke up. I was still thinking about my dream and its probable relation with Mig's sudden disappearance. I could find only one answer. This was the end of Swadhya. Mig was no more. He was dead. Only there guys were left now. The fourth was gone. I couldn't tell Armi and Jerry about Mig's death although I was quite sure of the fact. This news would break them. Slowly, I got up onto my feet. A drop of tear rolled down my cheeks.

"Why are you crying?" Jerry asked. I had no answer.

We headed straight for the Pushpanjali hospital where Mig was admitted by the police after he was found in an unconscious state hanging upside down from the Jamuna Bridge. He was quickly led to the ICU.

"I cannot assure you anything at the moment. There are just slim chances of his survival. He had taken a high dose of Nembutal and tried to commit suicide by jumping off a bridge" the doctor said on being about the chances of his survival.

Deep inside my heart was beating faster. I knew he wouldn't survive. My dream told me that. Jerry was meditating. Armi looked sad and depressing. I was helpless. Could I have prevented Mig from dying? The guilt was killing me.

"*Sab theek ho jayega*" one of the doctors told me.

"He had jumped of the bridge but his feet got entangled in one of the ropes connecting the mainstays. That was a miracle. The Jamuna would have washed him away if his feet wouldn't have got stuck" the doctor continued.

I flashed a weak smile at him. "Thank you" I said.

Another doctor came out of the ICU. "He's still not out of danger" he said.

Dusk turned into night but there was still no indication that Mig's condition had become stable. I and Armi fell asleep while Jerry continued his vigil.

At the crack of dawn, a doctor came up to Jerry. "His condition is stable now. He's out of danger. He will regain his consciousness in a while and then you can meet him" the doctor said.

"When will he be discharged" I asked.

"He'll need another day's rest and then he'll be completely fine" he said. I was elated. May be I was being a pessimist all this time. My premonition was proved wrong. I thanked the Lord. Dreams are just dreams.

An hour later Mig finally regained consciousness. We stepped inside the ICU.

"I'm sorry" he muttered.

"Why did you have to do this?" Jerry asked. Mig didn't reply. Only I know the reason but I kept silent.

There was just two days before our flight to Guwahati from where we would reach Shillong. Mig had almost recuperated and Jerry wouldn't let him come along with us.

"I want to start my life anew" Mig snapped Jerry as he tried to pacify him.

"Are you sure you can perform along with us?" Jerry asked.

"Of course Jerry, I can and I will" he replied. Mig was adamant.

Since the last two days we had practiced harder than ever. Sitting in a posh lounge in the Indira Gandhi International airport, we were waiting for our flight to arrive. It had been a long journey for the four of us. We came from nowhere only to become one of India's leading bands. We had achieved success in such a short period of time. May be, we were destined to be the pioneers of rock music in the country.

The flight landed exactly at 3 P.M at the Gopinath Bordoloi International airport in Guwahati. The organizers had arranged a cab for us to take us to Shillong. The serene Brahmaputra had dried up as it usually does during winters and the Brahmaputra Beach festival was on. Home smelt good. Guwahati had changed since the last time I was here. As we drove through the busy G.S. Road, the number of shopping malls and multiplexes on either side of the road amazed me. Guwahati was prospering. As we passed by my academy building, Rajeeta flashed back in my mind. What I was and what I had become. I laughed at myself.

After a two hour drive, we reached Umiam. Armi and Jerry had never seen the Umiam Lake before and when the beautiful sight emerged in front of their eyes, both of them screamed in delight.

"I think this is the real Scotland" Armi remarked.

The water of the lake reflected back the sun's rays making it look like the sky itself. It was set amidst hills on all sides and the small glistening waves hit the shore surrounded by pine trees. The pristine beauty was unmatched.

"I would definitely bring Ayushi to Shillong someday" Armi said. He was mesmerized.

I ordered the driver to stop the car by the side of a narrow opening which led to the shore below. We climbed downhill. I touched the cold water and I was instantly reminded of my childhood days when dad brought me here every weekends.

"This is heaven" Jerry remarked.

Jerry sang the beautiful MLTR song 'The animals' and I soon joined in with the chorus. Swadhya's voice echoed through the hills. Even the pine trees stood still as they listened to Swadhya's song.

It was almost dark when we reached Shillong. Hotel Polo Towers was a three star hotel where we would stay for the night. Temperatures had dropped and cozy beds welcomed us. I fell asleep as I lay on the bed. There was still sixteen hours before we would be onstage along with the Scorpions.

I woke up perspiring. I checked out my watch. It showed 4:30 A.M. The same dream haunted me again. As days were passing by, the frequency of the dream was increasing. I could not understand and neither did I want to. Swadhya's biggest concert was just twelve hours away. I decided to sleep.

The Polo ground was jam packed with around 70,000 people. It was 5:30 in the evening and was growing dark. It was raining. The crowd was growing every second. People from all over India were pouring in to watch the legends perform. It was estimated that around one lakh people would be watching the concert live in Shillong. It was a proud moment for all the north-easterners as Swadhya would open their show.

Backstage, Swadhya had its first brush with the members of Scorpions. I was impressed by the humility of the band members. They were huge stars but I couldn't see an iota of pride in them.

"We like Swadhya" Klaus Maine said to me as I went over to him for an autograph.

It was show time. Almost the entire crowd had assembled. Swadhya stepped on stage. This was the largest gathering I had ever witnessed in my life. It was pouring now. But even the rain Gods failed to dent people from watching the once in a lifetime concert. Shillong welcomed us with a loud cheer.

"Folks of this wonderful city, tonight we welcome one of the legendary bands of all times, please welcome, the Scorpions" I announced on the microphone.

Klaus Maine and Rudolf Schenker stepped on the stage first followed by the other members. They took a bow and left. The audience welcomed them with a huge round of applause.

"Folks, if you haven't recognized us yet, this is Swadhya, opening for the Scorpions live tonight" I continued.

The crowd roared. I felt elated. "Here goes our first song, 'Winds of change" I announced.

As soon as I had completed my sentence, the lights went off. I started whistling the tune of the song. As soon as I had completed, Jerry started on the lead and the lights flashed back. I started singing.

I follow the Moskva down to Gorky Park
Listening to the wind of change
An August summer night Soldiers passing by
Listening to the wind of change

The world is closing in did you ever think
That we could be so close, like brothers
The futures in the air I can feel it everywhere
Blowing with the wind of change

Take me to the magic of the moment
On a glory night
Where the children of tomorrow dream away
In the wind of change

The crowd was enjoying every moment of the show. I could see at the distance, people screaming and whistling. Some were jostling for space as they tried to get a clear view. Some were busy recording the performance on their mobile phones while some sang along with us.

Walking down the street distant memories
Are buried in the past forever
I follow the Moskva Down to Gorky Park
Listening to the wind of change

Take me to the magic of the moment
On a glory night
Where the children of tomorrow share their dreams
With you and me
Take me to the magic of the moment
On a glory night
Where the children of tomorrow dream away
In the wind of change

The wind of change
Blows straight into the face of time
Like a storm wind that will ring the freedom bell
For peace of mind
Let your balalaika sing
What my guitar wants to say

Take me to the magic of the moment

On a glory night
Where the children of tomorrow share their dreams
With you and me
Take me to the magic of the moment
On a glory night
Where the children of tomorrow dream away
In the wind of change

"We love you, Shillong" I screamed out on the microphone. This time a louder shout of approval went out from the crowd and it drained the sound of my voice. I ended the song and the audience appreciated us by clapping their hands in rhythm, in unison.

"Swadhya would now perform for you one of our own creations which will hit the stands along with our debut album 'The Resurrected Four'. I announced.

Jerry started on the lead while Armi and Mig joined in a few seconds later. We were singing the same song which we had performed in the grand finale of Band-It. It was 'When I held your hand'. Since it was a love ballad, people loved it instantly. The slight drizzle added to the charisma. No other band had enjoyed such a reception before.

"Shillong has always been my second home. I was born here and spent my entire childhood running in these misty hills in the midst of pine trees" I announced in the middle of the song.

"Swadhya, Swadhya...." I could hear Swadhya's name being cheered all around.

Our performance ended and we exited the stage. The reaction of the crowd was something I had never anticipated. Swadhya had managed to win the hearts of Shillong.

Soon the Scorpions stepped on stage and as they began performing.

One thing that came into my mind was 'they are Gods' and 'we are still nerds'.

After two and a half hour the show ended and we went back to the hotel.

What I never knew was the fact that dreams were not just dreams.

The Final Showdown

The Scorpions experience was exhilarating. Both Klaus Maine and Rudolf Schenker had called me up personally congratulating Swadhya for their magnificent performance. They even invited us for a performance in Germany along with Rammstein-the most popular German heavy metal band known for their songs 'Du hast' and 'Rosen rot'.

More people knew me now. Guwahati was proud of me. Swadhya's debut album, 'The Resurrected Four' was almost ready to hit the stands. We had recorded around ninety percent of the album and we had planned to wrap up the album in the next few weeks.

"Vodka and Shillong, wow! What can be more a lethal combination than this" Armi said.

It was time for celebrations. I could feel that Armi was a little disappointed but I didn't know the reason. He was a master in hiding emotions. The four of us were sitting in a pub. Rain hadn't stopped pouring since the time we had arrived here. This was our last night in Shillong and the four of us had decided to drink the night out.

Armi had guzzled almost seven glasses of Vodka and I could smell trouble.

"Something is wrong here. I can sense it" Armi said. Jerry looked at me.

"Armi, there is nothing here. You are drunk" I said.

"My intuitions are never wrong and you know it" Armi said almost sneering at me. Mig laughed aloud.

"Why are north-Indians so superstitious? I mean, I have seen almost everyone believing in black cats, sneezes, empty buckets and what not" Mig said.

"Don't you interrupt me when I'm talking" Armi said, pointing at Mig. Trouble was brewing. Jerry pacified Mig.

"Don't you talk bad about north-Indians? I mean, I never got due credit for my performance though I've worked as much hard as you did" Armi said.

This was the last thing that I wanted to happen. I knew that at some stage, someone would brag about credits but I never anticipated that this would happen so early. The verbal duel was unnecessary. I signaled Armi to cool down his flaring temper.

"Shut up, just a year ago you didn't know what a guitar was and now you are blabbering" Mig said as Jerry tried to stop him. This was getting worse.

"Stop it, Mr. Hermaphrodite; I don't want to see your damned face" Armi said. I had to stop this. I got up and pushed Armi behind. He got up with a jerk and punched Mig straight in his face before I could stop him. Before I could do anything Mig and Armi were embroiled in an abusive verbal duel

"I'll kill you, Mr. Hermaphrodite" Armi screamed.

The waiters arrived and both of them were restrained and segregated. Armi's intuition had once again proved to be correct.

"Why did you have to fight? He isn't a hermaphrodite" I said to Armi as Jerry led Mig away.

"He started it. I don't like that guy. He's an asshole" Armi said.

I knew Armi was drunk and the egotist in him had one again appeared. I wondered if he really hated Mig. The last thing I wanted was a break up. We had vowed to be a part of Swadhya whatever the situation was and I wondered if the two remembered their promises.

I left Armi alone. I could not approve Armi calling Mig a hermaphrodite. He wasn't a hermaphrodite. I accompanied Mig and Jerry. I was tired after drinking and I decided to sleep

The alarm sounded. It was 8:30 in the morning. We had to reach Guwahati in four hours. We had a return flight to Delhi. Jerry and Mig had already woken up and were packing their stuff. I went up to Armi's room only to find it locked. He was nowhere to be seen. This was weird. I went up to the reception where I was told that he had already checked out. My head almost spun when I heard this. Instead of reconciliation Armi was aggravating the situation.

"I'll stay behind at Guwahati for some days" Mig said.

"But why?" I asked.

"I want to spend some time with Nisha" he said.

"It's fine" I said. I was relieved that leaving the band wasn't in his mind. But I was crossed with Armi. He had left us alone.

In half an hour we were on our way to Guwahati. Guwahati made me feel nostalgic. This was the city where I had started dreaming. This city had taught me to dream. After a four hour flight and a three hour cab drive we finally reached Agra. Jerry went back to his apartment and I headed towards the hostel. I still had no idea where Armi was. On the way to my room, I found Armi's room unlocked. He had arrived here before us. I opened the door slowly. He was sitting on a chair, his head drooped down.

"I do not want to be a part of Swadhya anymore" he said, as soon as

I entered inside the room.

"But why?" I said.

"The three of you took all the credits. The north-easterners shower praise only to their own people. No one cares about a north-Indian" Armi said.

"It's not that Armi" I said.

"Whatever be the case, I won't work with Mig" he said. I said nothing. I left him alone.

A week later I received a call.

"We will offer you 2.5 million rupees for a gig at Guwahati" the voice said.

The offer was hard to resist but I had to consult the other members too before agreeing to the deal.

"I need some time" I said. He promised he would call me the following week and also promised to increase the amount if we demanded.

The problem was Armi. He still wasn't talking to me. He was in no mood to relent. It seemed that he had really developed hatred for the north-easterners and particularly for Mig. I somehow had to bring him back. That evening, I was passing by his room when I heard Armi yelling at someone on the phone.

"I'll pay you 25,000 but get that guy out of my way" he said in an obvious reference to Mig or I thought so. I was freaked out. *Who was he talking about? Was he paying supari for Mig?* I barged into his room.

"You are paying *supari*, aren't you?" I asked.

"Stay out of my business" he snapped back.

"If anything happens to Mig, I'll not forgive you" I said and walked out of his room. I knew I couldn't do anything. I couldn't believe the fact that Armi, who had once vowed to remain my best friend had turned to be my foe. Mig had still not returned and I felt that his life was in danger. Depression was killing Mig and now Armi was paying *supari* for him. I decided to wait for sometime before lodging a police complaint against my once-upon-a-time best friend.

Fifteen days had passed since I had last spoken to Armi. Although we lived in the adjacent rooms, it seemed that we were miles apart. Swadhya would achieve another milestone. Rock Street had decided to award us a shield of honour for our outstanding performance during the Scorpions concert. The organizers of the Guwahati gig called me up again.

"Sir, it has been more then fifteen days but you haven't reverted to me your decision. We were waiting" he said.

"I'm sorry, we won't be able to do the concert" I said.

"It's fine, but do let me know if you anytime want to alter your decision" he said. I felt he let off a sigh of dejection. I was crestfallen. I cut the line. I had lost all hope of reconciliation. It seemed that Swadhya's end was near. I had called up Mig everyday since I heard Armi and his *supari* conversation.

"Loneliness and vodka isn't much of a great combination" I said to myself as I ordered two glasses of the white alcohol.

This was the first time I was venturing out alone in the same old M.K Bar. I looked at the manager. The sneering smile was missing. Even he had sympathies for the great Samarth.

We had still not completed recording the entire album and the bosses were calling me up every few days to know when we would be available. '*Swadhya is gone*' I would say to myself. We were missing deadlines after deadlines. My instincts told me that our album would get scrapped although they always proved to be wrong every time Armi was around.

"Two glasses of Vodka for you, sir. Would you like to take anything else" the waiter asked as he put the glasses down on the table.

"A plate of *paneer pakodas* please" I requested. The waiter nodded.

Swadhya was my dream and it had come true. I didn't want to loose Swadhya nor any of my buddies. They were just too dear to me.

"A plate of *paneer pakodas* for you Sir" the waiter said. I was impressed. The waiter was extraordinarily well behaved.

Within minutes, I had guzzled down the entire drink. I ordered for more. Alcohol might not be the answers to all the questions but alcohol definitely helps to forget all those questions. The waiter brought me two more drinks. I gulped them down as well.

The room seemed to spin and twirl. My vision got blurred and I felt someone pushing his hands through my pockets. I lay my head on the table and I passed out.

The alarm sounded. My vision was still blurred and dizziness had still not settled in. I was in my room. I had been sleeping all night long. I tried to recall what might have happened the night before but I couldn't.

"You are no competition to me in drinking" a voice said.

I rubbed my eyes. I could see Armi giggling. I jumped out of the bed and hugged him. Armi had returned. This was Swadhya's resurrection.

"What happened the night before?" I said. I was curious to know how he had landed in the bar.

"I had come there for a drink and I saw you lying in an unconscious state. The waiter was trying to rob you. I thrashed him and I carried you back to the hostel and here you are now lying in a pitiable state" Armi said.

"Thanks" I said.

"So when are we recording our last song?" Armi asked.

I quickly picked up my phone and dialed my bosses' number.

"We are available tomorrow to record our last song" I said.

Mig finally arrived from Guwahati in the evening. He had been shuttling between Guwahati and Shillong where he had put up in the same hotel where we were lodged during the Scorpions concert to avoid the risk of being assassinated.

I and Armi was sitting, discussing our plans for our next recording when Mig entered my room along with Jerry. I could sense that Armi was ashamed of his deeds. He wouldn't look up to Mig. I poked him, signaling him to ask sorry for what he had done.

Mig sat beside me while Jerry sat on the chair beside the computer.

"I'm sorry, Mig" Armi said. Mig smiled and nodded, acknowledging his apology.

"Being sorry doesn't help. I was ruining myself all this time" Armi said.

"Asking sorry is far more a greater deed than hitting someone" Mig said.

I never knew Mig had the spirit of Mahatma Gandhi inside him. Nevertheless, all's well that ends well. Mig and Armi shook their hands while I hugged the two. Swadhya would rock once again.

"Well done boys" the boss screamed out as we finished recording our final song. The 'Resurrected Four' was ready to hit the music stores. In the train back to Agra, I called up the organizers of the Guwahati gig.

"We are ready to perform at home" I said.

"Thank you so much, sir" the voice answered back.

"We will finalize the dates in a couple of days" I said.

"It's fine sir, thank you once again" the voice said. I cut the line. I turned towards the three.

"An organizer in Guwahati is paying us 2.5 million bucks for a concert there" I said. Armi's eyes almost popped out.

"2.5 million bucks? You are kidding, aren't you?" Armi asked.

I was finding it hard to resist 2.5 million bucks and so was Armi. But I had doubts if Mig would agree to it. He had a record of not performing with any band that humiliated him and made him feel like an outsider.

"I'm in" Jerry said.

"But I've doubts" Mig said. I knew Mig would find it difficult to agree but I decided to convince him.

"You know me Samarth; I find it very difficult to perform alongside people who don't respect my sentiments and raise a hue and cry about my personal life" Mig said

My first attempt had backfired. Nevertheless, I decided to give it another shot. I could only hope that Mig would somehow change his mind.

The 'Resurrected Four' finally hit the music stores fifteen days after we had recorded the final song. Our debut album in its opening day sold

a massive five thousand copies. That was a record. No other Indian rock band had sold as many copies as Swadhya did in its opening day. It became a rage even in Agra. We were promoted. From being stars, we were now superstars.

We were in for huge surprise when Ankit and Bodu threw in a grand party for us. This party had everything in it- from booze to boobs.

"I even thought of inviting strippers" Ankit said when asked why he had invited pole dancers to the party. There was free beer, free pizzas and free abuses as well. In the midst of the party, I received a call.

"Sir, you haven't finalized the dates for the concert yet" the voice said.

"Can you please hold on for a minute" I said.

"Sure sir" he said.

Mig had still not agreed to perform at Guwahati. I decided to give it a last shot.

"Cummon Mig, you have to do it; does it mean that you haven't forgiven Armi yet? He is willing to ask forgiveness again if you want; Past has passed" I said, echoing the words which Megha had once said to me.

Mig shook his head. I was disappointed.

"At least do it for Nisha. She will be proud of you" I said.

I knew I was blackmailing him emotionally but I had no other options left. Mig sat down. I could sense that he was in a delirium.

"Okay, I'll do it" Mig said after a brief pause. I hugged him.

"Thanks brother" I said. Mig had finally relented. I felt happier. I got back on the phone.

"What about the 30th of this month?" I said.

"It would be great Sir" the voice said.

"Then 30th be it" I said.

"Thank you so much Sir" he said.

"One more thing that I need you to tell you is that the security should be tight at the venue" I said. Guwahati had a history of massive bomb blasts by underground rebels and I didn't wasn't to take a chance.

"Definitely sir, I would make sure that the security is stringent" he said. I cut the line.

The plane landed at the Gopinath Bordoloi International airport exactly at 10:30 A.M. The organizers had already booked a hotel for us. Nisha was waiting at the airport. I decided to spend a little time at home. Mom wanted to know more about the girl I was going around with. The last time I told her about Shreya, she offered me an unconditional offer that I could marry my choice only if I pass my engineering and get a fair job with a handsome package. Now that I had piled up too many backlogs and Shreya no longer in my life, the probability of her decision going against me was getting bleak. Dad was still crossed with me for my '*gaana-bajana*'.

The final year of engineering was proving to be tough for Armi. The last fifteen days were tougher. The netas had formed a lobbying group to get Armi rusticated from college. Their leader was Sunil Singh. That was when I came to know that Sunil Singh had threatened Armi of dire consequences if Armi stood in their way and Armi had almost made plans to get him killed. That was what the *supari conversation* was all about. I was relieved when I heard that Armi had never planned to kill Mig.

We came out of the airport. A young girl dressed in a pink top and a blue Capri came running towards us. I was bewildered until she embraced Mig. Nisha was looking gorgeous. I saw Nisha whispering something into his ears. Mig came towards me and introduced her to the three of us.

"I have finally decided to surrender" Mig said. I looked into his twinkling eyes.

"It's your decision, Mig" I said, as I picked up my luggage from the conveyor belt.

While I was talking to Mig, I saw Armi sneaking behind a pretty young lasso to catch a glimpse of her. He was still the same old Armaan Sharma.

"I'll start my life anew" Mig said. Love had changed him.

As we walked out of the airport, a member of the organizing committee, who he introduced himself as Joy Sen, welcomed us. We were led to a waiting car.

"Straight to the police station" Joy ordered the driver as we sat inside the cab. I was bewildered. *Police station? We had committed no crime.*

"Why police station?" I asked.

"Stringent security measures" he answered.

After a ten minutes drive, we reached the police station.

We were provided with a police convoy consisting of gun totting commandoes on two cars-one at the back and one at the front. We were sandwiched but for the first time in my life I felt like a VIP. I felt I had the power to anything and everything.

Everything said and done, we drove straight to the hotel. There were still 24 hours before the final showdown.

The venue was the Judges Field. The stadium wasn't as large as the one in which we had performed during the Scorpions concert, but we couldn't complain because we were performing at home. The ground could hold no less than 10,000 people and we had planned a grand surprise for the home crowd.

As we entered the ground, a slight drizzle welcomed us. Rain at home tasted sweet. A full capacity crowd was expected. It was almost 5 P.M and an hour later we would be on stage. We had decided to perform seven songs with the first one being the cover of 'Mama said', a Metallica song which incorporated country music and hard rock. I found the music soothing and the trio instantly agreed to it. Other than Mama said, we had also decided to perform three songs from our debut album, a cover of Def Leppard's 'When love and hate collide' and cover versions of Nirvana's 'Lake of fire' and 'Something in the way'.

Armi had already made a things-to-do list with the money he would receive after the show. He showed me the list. It was something like this.

Things to do:

1. A trip to Seychelles(with Ayushi)
2. Experience base jumping
3. A two day/three night trek on the Mt. Kilimanjaro
4. Feed polar bears
5. Spend a night at the Chillingham castle.

I wondered where he got those ideas from.

People were pouring in slowly. Backstage, we geared up for the grand show. Armi came up to me.

"I'm getting a bad feeling" Armi said. Armi was pissing me off.

"Look outside. What do you see?" I said. Armi peeped out through a small opening on one of the huge curtains.

"There are ten thousand fans waiting for us to step on stage. I mean, I won't like to disappoint ten thousand fans" I said.

"You know about my instincts, Samarth. It says that something terrible might happen" he said.

Jerry was tuning his guitar when I called him.

"Do you think that there is something wrong here" I asked Jerry.

"No, everything is fine. In fact, I'm enjoying the weather" Jerry said. I called up Mig too.

"Are you apprehensive about performing tonight?" I asked Mig.

"Absolutely not; Nisha has invited all of her friends to watch us perform tonight" Mig said. I turned back to Armi.

"Are you satisfied now Mr. Armaan?" I said.

"I still trust my instincts" Armi said.

"I'm sorry; I can allay your fears no more. It's entirely up to you whether you want to be a part of this show" I said. Armi shook his head.

"Okay, I'll do it" he said.

The clock struck seven and we stepped on stage. As expected, ten thousand fans had gathered to watch us perform. As we put our first steps, a huge cheer greeted us. I could see Nisha with her set of friends amongst the crowd. She was proud of Mig.

Prat and Dhritik had called me twice congratulating me for my success. Prat had landed a job in Sweden and so couldn't make it to the show. On the other hand, Dhritik's exams played spoilsport.

"Folks, thank you so much for coming here tonight and making this event a huge success. This is Swadhya's first show in Guwahati and we plan to perform again in the following month. It has always been my, in fact our dream to perform in this lovely city and it has finally come true. We plan to donate a part of our fees to an orphanage. Thank you once again" I announced on the microphone.

Jerry stated with the acoustic. I joined in soon after.

Mama, *she has taught me well*
Told me when I's young
Son, your life's an open book
Don't close it 'fore it's done
The brightest flame burns quickest
That's what I heard her say
A son's heart's owed to mother
But I must find my way

Let my heart go
Let your son grow
Mama, let my heart go
Or let this heart be still

Mama, now I'm coming home
I'm not all you wished of me
But a mother's love for her son
Unspoken, help me be
Oh Yeah I took your love for granted
And all the things you said to me
I need your arms to welcome me
But a cold stone's all I see

Mig and Armi joined in simultaneously. The crowd grew wild. Ten thousand people, screaming on top of their voices almost drained the music from the sound system. I could feel the energy, the vibe. I closed my eyes as I continued singing.

Let my heart go
Mama, let my heart go
You never let my heart go
So let this heart be still

Never I ask of you
What never I gave
But you gave me your emptiness
I now take to my grave
Never I ask of you
But never I gave
But you gave me your emptiness
I now take to my grave
So let this heart be still

The crowd sang along with me. Swadhya had done it once again. I looked at Jerry. He seemed to be in a trance.

"Thank you" I said, as we ended the song.

"Our next song is one of our original creations" I announced. Jerry started playing the soothing tune of 'When I held your hand'.

The intro sounded perfect. I visualized Shreya as I started singing the song. I could smell her, the perfume which she wore during my golden sojourn and the way we kissed. The way we had promised to be together forever. For a moment, I forgot the roaring crowd and the stage and Swadhya. Shreya besieged my mind. We ended the song and I returned from my reverie.

"It's better to burn out than to fade away" Mig announced.

A moment later I heard a gunshot. I turned around. Armi lay on the stage. Mig was nowhere to be seen. Jerry came running towards me. My mind reverberated with thoughts. *What happened?* I turned back again to see the crowd. They stood there in disbelief, in shock. Moments later, Armi stood up and I heaved a sigh of relief. Mig was probably alive too. We rushed towards him. Security officers came running. I broke out in sweat as I saw Mig. He lay there, blood oozing out of his forehead and a gun in his hand. I fell unconscious.

I woke up perspiring. I opened my eyes only to find myself surrounded by mom, dad, Jerry and Armi. I looked around. I was in a hospital. My left arm was bandaged.

"What....what happened?" I said.

Jerry burst out in tears. All the others kept silent.

"Will someone tell me what just happened?" I screamed, as I tried to lift myself up but my arms didn't support me. I lay back again.

"Mig is no more" Armi said.

I felt a lump in my throat. I felt choked and smothered. I closed my eyes. A large drop of tear rolled down my eyes.

Mig has committed suicide. The doctors tried to save him but the bulled punched a hole right inside his cerebrum. We brought you to the hospital." Armi said.

The story had ended. Swadhya's journey ended. If I had paid heed to Armi's advice this day would have never come. The past flashed back in my mind.

"I'm responsible for this mess. Armi had told me about the impending danger but I never listened to him" I said.

"No one is responsible, things happen because they have to happen" Armi said.

"It's all about destiny *beta*" dad added.

The guilt was killing me. If we wouldn't have performed tonight, Mig wouldn't have done this to him.

I realized the meaning of my dream. There were three guys on stage. The drummer was missing. Mig's favourite quote was 'Its better to burn out than to fade away' and so was Cobain's. In the dream, Cobain appeared and then disappeared and so had Mig. I was warned repeatedly but I could never comprehend its meaning. I thought Mig was an avatar of Cobain himself.

Mig was our hero. He would never fade away from our memories nor would Swadhya.

As I stood beside Mig's pyre watching it burn, I sensed Mig's presence. He would always be with us, everywhere. Soon after Mig's death we decided to never perform again. Without Mig, Swadhya would be a hollow twig. The phenomenal success that we had attained was all because of the great drummer-Mriganka Saikia.

Back at home, as I played a song from our album, I heard someone whispering into my ears- 'Its Better to Burn out Then to Fade Away'.

I smiled.

Epilogue

It was tough living life without Swadhya and Mig. Armi and I finally became engineers. After the debacle at Guwahati, I solely concentrated on my studies. I landed up a job in one of the prestigious MNC's while Armi left for the foreign shores to pursue his masters. Jerry applied for an audition for a foreign band and scraped through. He now plays the guitar for 'The Viking Lords', a U.S based band. He is still single.

Armi regularly practices with the likes of Rudolf Schenker and Paul H. Landers. You have guessed correctly. He has settled down in Germany. He is yet to marry Ayushi but his latest mail indicated that they would tie the knot soon.

Nisha is still single and she runs an orphanage along with working in the hospital. She has pledged her life in the service of mankind.

The weather was hot and humid. Even the powerful air conditioning failed to cool my burning body. I sat down on a cozy sofa, waiting, and my thoughts turned back two years ago. It was two years ago that I first met the love of my life-Shreya. You are right. She came back in my life.

A day before convocation, I received a mail.

Dear Samarth,

I'm really sorry to say that I can no longer continue our relationship. My parents have already chosen a boy and they want me to marry him. I cannot go against them. Sorry once again.

Regards

Megha

I broke up as I read the mail. Tears swelled up in my eyes. I would have banged my head on the wall if I hadn't received another mail.

Dear Samarth,

I've tried to run and hide but I'm no longer able to do so. No one can fill up the void that you have left behind. I had taken a very wrong decision and now I regret it. I want you to return. I love you and I always will.

Yourbeloved

Shreya

Yup! She had returned after a year's gap and there I was sitting in Barista waiting for her arrival. I had undertaken yet another golden sojourn.

Finally, Shreya entered. She held in her hand a small gift packet. I wondered what was inside it. She sat on the sofa beside me. I looked into her eyes.

"You are still the same" she said.

"I hate changes" I said. She handed me the box.

"What's inside it?" I asked.

"Unwrap and check" she said.

I opened the packet. My eyes fell on a piece of paper. I unfolded it. On one side she had written '*Ode to Love*' while on the other she wrote '*I miss you*'. I read the poem.

"I'm sorry" she said. I held her hand. She looked beautiful as ever.

"Past has passed, let the future roll" I said.

After much struggle, I finally found love. The trip to Fatehpur Sikri had borne fruits. I thanked the Lord.

I was sitting in my office checking my daily mails when I received a message. On opening my inbox, I found the message-

3 days to go; I'm in India
Waiting outside your office

The last line almost knocked my brains out. It was Jerry. I checked out the calendar. A year had passed since we had performed our last show. There was still three more days before Mig's first death anniversary. I wondered what Jerry had in his mind. I quickly walked outside.

"Hey brother, nice to see you again" I said. He was accompanied by a foreigner. I shook hands with him.

"This is Paul Newlands, drummer of the Viking Lords" Jerry said.

"Would you like to perform another show? I assure that this will be our last show" Jerry said.

"I don't think so. I have lost my voice" I said.

"The show will commemorate Mig's first death anniversary and the proceedings will go to Nisha's orphanage. Please, it's a request" Jerry said.

The fact was that I never wanted to return to the past. It still pained and guilt returned every time I thought about the final showdown.

"Okay, I'll do it but does anyone know where Armi is? I haven't received any mails from him since the past one week" I said, finally deciding that the performance would be for a good cause. I called up Armi.

"Hey fatass, where are you?" I said.

"Hey thinass, I am feeding polar beers" he answered. He was still a weirdo.

"So your dream has finally come true" I said.

“Yup, and I have a wife now” he said.

“What? You never told me that you have married Ayushi” I said.

“Now you know, actually we walked down the aisle here in Antarctica yesterday” he said.

“Congratulations! Would you like to perform another show?” I said, explaining to him the reasons.

“Sure, why not?” he said. Swadhya would rock for the last time.

As I took a stroll of the Judges Field, the place where Swadhya had performed their last show and where Mig fell, I felt my eyes get moist. I could feel Mig’s presence everywhere.

Nehru Stadium would be the host to Swadhya’s final show. Armi arrived with his wife. He had mastered the guitar.

The stadium was teeming with people. They had come to pay homage to Mig. We received a standing ovation as we put our first steps on the stage.

“It has been a year since we lost out dear friend Mriganka Saikia. We have come together commemorate his first death anniversary. This is our last show. The money generated through ticket sales will go to ‘Mriganka Saikia Memorial House’, an orphanage run by Nisha” I announced.

The crowd stood still while I said this.

For the next two and a half hours, we played Mig’s favourite songs and the crowd loved every moment. I would cherish every moment that I had spent with the three. I would treasure all the memories forever.

Many bands had achieved success in such a short period of time and achieve phenomenal success but not many bands could reside in people's hearts for long. Nirvana did and so did Swadhya. Swadhya would never fade away. After the show ended, I returned home.

I woke up perspiring. The same dream revisited me again. I was left clueless.